# Murder of a Judge

By

Gopal Ramanan

Printed in the United States of America

First Printing June 2019
Second Printing August 2019

ISBN: 9781070418322

This book is dedicated to the memory of my dear beloved wife Vidya,
who left our earthly abode far too soon.
"Vidya dearest, you will always be in my heart and soul"

Other books by the same author:

*It's All In The Stars & Other Stories*

# Chapter 1

A penetrative, repetitive sound was doing its best to drag Inspector Ashok Anand out of the depths of his deep slumber. He had gone to bed early that Saturday night, tired out from a long week spent running around in the hot and humid April weather, following up on cases and other tasks assigned to him. He felt as though he had fallen asleep just minutes ago. Opening his bleary eyes in sleepy half-consciousness, he saw that it was still dark outside his bedroom windows, so it couldn't be morning yet. What was it that had woken him up? Then his sleep-befuddled brain registered the insistent ringing of the telephone in the sitting room of his bungalow. He glanced at the illuminated display of the alarm clock on the side table by his bed. The hands of the clock pointed to 10:35 pm. No wonder it felt like he had just gone to sleep! For a few moments he was tempted to just remain there in his comfortable bed, let the phone keep ringing until it stopped, and go back to sleep. Then common sense prevailed. What if the call was about something important?

He reached out and switched on his bedside lamp, then got out of bed and made his way to the sitting room, where he turned on the lights. He sank wearily into the armchair next to the ringing telephone, lifted the receiver, and said: "Hello!"

"May I please speak to Inspector Ashok Anand?" enquired the voice at the other end.

"Speaking," responded the Inspector.

"Sir, this is Sub-Inspector Prakash at Police Headquarters. We received a call from one Balram Singh saying that his master has been shot dead."

That statement jolted Inspector Anand fully awake. "Give me the particulars," he said.

He heard a rustling of papers at the other end of the line. "We did not get much detail, sir," Prakash said apologetically. "This Balram Singh said that he had to attend to madam, and hung up."

Inspector Anand felt a surge of irritation. "Did he at least tell you where the shooting took place?" he snapped.

"Oh yes, sir, I managed to get that out of him," said Prakash, sounding pleased with himself. "It appears to have been at the judge's residence. I asked him for the address." Prakash read it out to him, and Inspector Anand jotted it down on a notepad he kept by the phone.

"Did this Balram Singh provide any other information?"

"No, sir. But in the background, I could hear a woman's voice crying. After giving me the address, Balram said that he had to attend to madam, and hung up."

Inspector Anand sighed. It appeared that his much-needed rest would have to be postponed. He said, "Prakash, please send a police jeep around to my house right away, with an extra constable in addition to the driver."

"Yes, sir. I will do so at once."

The Inspector replaced the receiver and sat pondering for a few moments. Even though it was now 1980, shooting deaths were still rare in Trivandrum. The majority of crime the police had to deal with concerned burglaries, domestic violence, drunken assaults, and missing persons, not murder.

He heaved himself tiredly to his feet, went back through his bedroom into the adjoining bathroom, splashed some cold water on his face, and toweled himself dry. He then returned to his bedroom and changed from the thin cotton kurta and pyjamas he had been wearing into his police inspector's uniform.

As he stood in front of the full-length mirror in his bedroom, adjusting the uniform, he felt a sense of pride, as he always did when he wore that khaki-colored outfit. To him, the uniform represented a symbol of his authority to protect the public and uphold the law of the land.

Inspector Anand turned away from the mirror and walked over to a large framed photograph hanging on the bedroom wall. It displayed a very pretty lady, clad in a red sari, smiling at him out of the picture. An overwhelming sadness swept through him: the photograph was of his beloved wife, who had passed away about two years ago. He extended his right hand, touched the image with his fingertips, and then dabbed his eyes, quietly murmuring a brief prayer. It was so painful for him to keep realizing that she was no longer with him; that he would never again feel the touch of her hand, nor hear the sound of her voice. Tears welled up in his eyes.

Trying hard to control his emotions, Inspector Anand went into his kitchen and made himself a cup of tea. He decided to wait outside for the arrival of the police jeep. Carrying his tea-cup, he unbolted the front door and stepped out onto his front veranda, turning on the porch light, and closed and locked the front door behind him.

He sat down in one of the two wicker chairs set out on the covered front veranda, facing the garden. The relative coolness at that time of night was a welcome relief after the heat of the day, and the air was fragrant with the scent of jasmine flowers growing in profusion in his front garden. He considered himself fortunate to own an independent bungalow, a legacy from his late father. It was not large, but he and his wife had found it spacious enough for their needs. He preferred to live here rather than at the crowded multi-story police staff quarters, because his bungalow had a nice-sized garden, both front and back, that he liked to potter about in, tending to his plants, whenever he had the time. He loved gardening, like his late father before him, and found it to be a great stress reliever.

Sipping his chai, Inspector Anand pondered on the upcoming case. He had little detail to go on at this point, except that someone had been shot dead at his residence. He wondered what events had led to this particular crime. Robbery? A domestic dispute? Oh well, it was useless to speculate without more facts. He recalled wryly that in one of the Sherlock Holmes stories that he used to read so avidly when he was a teenager, the famous detective had said: "It is a capital mistake to theorize before you have all the evidence."

Inspector Anand's train of thought was interrupted by the arrival of the police jeep, which pulled up with a squeal of brakes outside his front gate. As he climbed on to the passenger seat next to the driver, he noted with dismay that the constable assigned to him tonight, seated in the back seat, was Varghese, a mournful man who went through life with unwavering pessimism and gloom. Constable Varghese gave him a half-hearted salute, and said: "A shooting death, Inspector! What is Trivandrum coming to? Going to the dogs, Inspector, going to the dogs!" He heaved a heavy sigh and shook his head sadly.

"Yes, yes," said Inspector Anand hurriedly, and before Varghese could add to his gloomy refrain, he turned to the driver, young Constable Kurian, and asked: "Do you know the address we are going to?"

"Yes, Inspector."

"Then let's go."

The police jeep sped through the undulating hilly streets of the town. There was little traffic at that time of night. Inspector Anand reflected that the march of so-called progress had done little to change the somnolent nightlife of Trivandrum. The majority of shops and restaurants shut their doors by 9:00 or 9:30 pm, and most of the residents were indoors even earlier. A senior police official, visiting from Bombay, had snorted disgustedly: "Trivandrum is like a big village! You policemen here have it easy. Why, at 10:00 pm in Bombay, we are just getting started!" This official was a pompous man and such statements were typical of him. Inspector Anand had been irritated by his remark and had pointed out that residents appreciated the fact that Trivandrum was on the whole a peaceful city, a picturesque green metropolis renown for its beautiful old buildings, temples, museums, and lovely white beaches.

# Chapter 2

They arrived at their destination some fifteen minutes later. It turned out to be an old two-story house, standing independently in a large lot surrounded by high walls on all sides. It was located on a quiet street of similar homes in one of the older residential areas of the city. Tall and wide iron gates provided entry into the compound.

The top of the gatepost on the right side of the front gates had a triangular metal plaque built into the concrete, inscribed with the words "Judge Mohan Pillai". Inspector Anand recognized the name. Mohan Pillai was a formidable, sharp-tongued District & Sessions Court judge with a reputation for handing out harsh sentences to criminals. He was generally considered to be honest and incorruptible, albeit with a short temper that brooked no nonsense from those unlucky enough to appear in his court.

7

The police jeep pulled up in front of the big iron gates and Inspector Anand climbed out, followed by Constable Varghese. A weather beaten wrinkled old man wearing a khaki shirt and trousers came hurrying up and unbolted and swung open the big gates. From his dress and appearance, the Inspector guessed that he was probably one of the servants of the household, most likely the watchman. He thanked the old man and walked up the broad gravel drive, Constable Varghese following behind him. A clean and well polished white Ambassador sedan stood in the driveway. Parked behind stood an orange colored two-wheel Vespa scooter.

To the left of the driveway was the front garden, with a neatly trimmed lawn. Large oleander bushes covered with pink and white flowers grew densely next to the high wall that separated the garden from the street and sidewalk outside.

From the driveway, a narrow gravel path ran parallel to the front of the house, and ended at a short flight of broad concrete steps which led up to a wide covered veranda, supported by large white pillars that flanked the steps leading up from the front garden.

Beyond the veranda's six foot depth was a wide doorway with double wooden doors that were standing open. There were lights burning in the room beyond, and Inspector Anand could hear the sound of voices inside. He crossed the veranda and paused in the doorway, asking Varghese to wait just outside the entrance.

The Inspector found himself gazing into a large rectangular room, furnished with a long sofa, a low long wooden table in front of the sofa, and two armchairs, one at each end of the rectangular table. Paintings by the famous Kerala painter Ravi Varma were hung on the walls. Overhead, a ceiling fan whirred quietly, providing a welcoming breeze in the sultry night.

To the left of the sitting area was the dining room, furnished with a large oval-shaped dining table with six chairs arranged around it. There was a doorway on the right-hand side of the dining room; he subsequently discovered that it led to the kitchen. To the right of the sitting area was an angular staircase with balustrades, which presumably led to the upper storey of the house.

The Inspector's dark, somber eyes surveyed the occupants of the room. Standing behind one of the armchairs, with his arms folded across his chest, was a very tall, broad-shouldered Sikh wearing an orange kurta and khaki slacks. Inspector Anand was tall himself — his height had been measured at six feet — but the Sikh appeared to be a good five to six inches taller. He had a muscular body and deepset calm almond-shaped eyes, and most of his face was covered by a big beard and mustache streaked with gray. On his head, covering his hair, he wore a tightly wound turban, in keeping with the traditions of the Sikh people.

Seated in one of the armchairs was a thin youth wearing a light blue short-sleeve shirt and grey trousers. He had thick wavy black hair that fell over his forehead, a long narrow face, and a neatly trimmed beard, and if it weren't for his sullen expression, could even be called handsome. He was staring defiantly at a middle aged lady seated in the other armchair. She was dressed in a simple beige-colored sari with a dark border. Her dark hair was neatly plaited and hung down her back. The lady's round face was streaked with tears and her eyes were red and swollen.

Catching sight of the tall, lean uniformed figure standing in the doorway, the middle aged lady exclaimed: "At last! The Police have arrived!"

Stepping forward, Inspector Anand said: "Mrs. Pillai?"

"Yes! Yes! I am Mrs. Pillai!" she replied, with a touch of impatience.

"Madam, I am Inspector Ashok Anand of the Trivandrum Police CID. One Balram Singh telephoned us about someone in this house being shot?"

"Yes, Inspector — it is my husband Mohan who has been shot! Murdered!" Her voice broke and tears ran down her cheeks.

"Please accept my condolences, madam," Inspector Anand said sincerely. "It must be very difficult for you at this time." He knew, even as he spoke the words, how formal they must sound. He had often felt that this was one of the hardest parts of a police officer's job, to commiserate with the next of kin and other relatives, knowing that nothing that was said could adequately address their bereavement. He waited patiently until she appeared to have regained some measure of control. Then he asked, gently: "Could you tell me who these two people are?" He indicated the tall Sikh and the youth.

Mrs. Pillai wiped her eyes with the edge of her sari, and gesturing towards the tall Sikh, she said: "This is Balram Singh, Inspector. He has been my husband's faithful driver and bodyguard for over twenty years."

Balram Singh put the palms of his hands together and bowed in the Inspector's direction. Inspector Anand acknowledged the gesture with a brief nod. As a rule, he liked the Sikh people; he had generally found them to be honest, hardworking, and loyal. His impression of people he saw for the first time were usually strong, bringing with it a perception of their character. But at this point, until he gathered more evidence, he did not want to prejudge any of the occupants of the house.

Indicating the thin youth seated in the armchair, Mrs. Pillai continued, "And this is my husband's nephew Thakshak."

Thakshak looked nervous and frightened. His eyes flickered up for a brief instant to meet the Inspector's gaze, then dropped to resume staring at the polished tile floor at his feet.

Turning to Mrs. Pillai, Inspector Anand asked: "Where is the murder victim, madam?"

"In the office room," Mrs. Pillai replied. "Balram, please show the Inspector. I prefer not to go in there again." She leaned back in her chair with a shudder and closed her eyes.

"Please follow me, Inspector sahib," Balram Singh said. He stepped past Inspector Anand and out of the front door on to the veranda and led the way along the veranda towards a room that jutted out into the front garden. The door was shut, and Balram opened it and the Inspector followed him inside.

It was a square room of medium size. The Inspector's attention was immediately drawn to the body of a tall, thin old man slumped back in an armchair behind a large wooden desk in the middle of the room. He had silver-gray hair brushed back from a high forehead, a long narrow face, prominent nose, and thin lips pressed firmly together. Even in death, the face looked stern and gave off an appearance of strength, coupled with a hint of arrogance.

Inspector Anand stepped forward and scrutinized the body closely. Early on in his career, he had dreaded the sight of a corpse, especially when the death had been unnatural. Perhaps it was the thought that the person would never move or talk again, that what was once a living, breathing human being was now just a body, a mass of flesh and bones. But over the years, he had trained himself not to flinch at the sight of death, recognizing that it went hand in hand with his profession.

The judge was wearing a white kurta and crisply starched dhoti, and across the front of the kurta, in the region of his heart, was a large crimson stain. The Inspector peered closer and saw that there was a round hole in the kurta, no doubt made by a bullet. The area around the small hole was sticky with congealing blood. A blood-soaked towel lay on the floor beside the armchair.

Inspector Anand prowled around the room. The judge's large wooden desk faced a wide window that looked out into the front garden. It had firmly embedded vertical iron bars running top to bottom. This was a common security feature of older houses all over Kerala; it provided an effective deterrent to would-be burglars. The front of the desk stood about ten feet away from the window. Two wooden armchairs with cane seats faced the desk.

The wall to the left of the entrance door was lined with tall wooden bookshelves filled with imposing looking hardbound volumes. Set in the wall across from the the entrance doorway was another door which led to a small bathroom equipped with a western-style toilet and washbasin with tap.

The Inspector noted that the doorway he had come through from the veranda appeared to be the only entrance and exit for the office room.

Telling Balram that he was finished with his inspection of the office room for the time being, Inspector Anand stepped outside onto the broad veranda with the tall Sikh, asked him to close the door, went over to the police jeep and called police headquarters over the two-way radio, requesting a forensics team to be sent over, giving them the address.

# Chapter 3

There were two cane-and-bamboo chairs on the front veranda. Inspector Anand sat down in one, pulled out his notebook, and said to Balram Singh, "I want go over what happened this evening. You can sit, if you wish," he added, and gestured towards the other chair.

"Thank you, Inspector sahib, but I prefer to stand."

Inspector Anand looked him over. Arms folded across his chest, Balram Singh held himself upright, his back ramrod straight, like a military man. The eyes below the neatly wound turban were deep-set and calm.

"Very well. To begin with, what were you doing around the time of the murder?"

"I was in the kitchen, eating my evening meal," Balram replied. "It is customary for me to eat there after the family has finished eating in the dining room and my wife has cleared the dining table and brought the remaining food back into the kitchen."

"Your wife, Balram? So she works here also?"

"Yes, Inspector sahib. She is the cook and maid servant here."

"I see. So you were eating your dinner. And then?"

"I heard a lot of angry shouting going on in the office room."

"The kitchen is behind the dining room, correct?" interrupted Inspector Anand.

"Yes, Inspector sahib."

"That means that it is towards the back of the house. But you were still able to hear what was going on in the office room?"

"If the talking is being done in a normal tone, I cannot hear," Balram explained. "But tonight, with the kitchen window and the office room window both being open, I could hear the sound of angry voices, although I could not make out what was being said. I was surprised, because even when Judge sahib has a visitor in there, voices are seldom raised. Then I thought, it's none of my business, perhaps Judge sahib is very angry at someone, so I continued with my meal. Then there was a sharp 'crack!' sound like a car backfiring, and I heard the judge cry out, as if in pain."

"Around what time was this?" asked Inspector Anand.

"I cannot be entirely sure, Inspector Sahib," said Balram apologetically. "I was eating and not paying much attention to the time."

"Can you make a guess as to the approximate time when you heard the judge cry out?"

"I think it was around 9:15 pm."

The Inspector made a quick entry in his notebook, and said, "And then what did you do?"

"I immediately jumped to my feet, washed my hands at the kitchen tap, and ran through the dining room and then through the living room to the front veranda." Balram paused and added, "That is the quickest way to get to the office room from the kitchen, Inspector sahib. One could also go through the back door of the kitchen to the rear courtyard, then around the side of the house to the front, but that is a more roundabout way."

"I understand," Inspector Anand said. "And then what did you do?"

"I knocked on the door to the office room and called out, asking if everything was all right. When I received no answer, I tried to open the door, but it would not open. It appeared to be bolted from the inside."

"Was that normal, for the office door to be bolted like that while the judge was inside?"

"No, most definitely not. Judge sahib would sometimes close the office door when he had someone in there with him, but he would never bolt it. And when he sat alone in the office room, which he did on most evenings, he never even closed the door."

"I see. Please go on."

"So I pounded on the office door and shouted. Meanwhile, Mrs. Pillai joined me and said that Thakshak was in there as well."

Inspector Anand interrupted him, asking sharply: "Thakshak — the nephew — was in the office room with Judge Pillai?"

"Yes, Inspector sahib. That is what madam said when we were standing outside the office door."

The Inspector drew a deep breath. Whatever he had expected, it was not this. He was tempted to immediately go into the sitting room and question the nephew. But no, he told himself. Let me finish questioning this tall sardar first. No point jumping back and forth from one witness to the next like a jack-in-the-box.

He said: "Do you know when Thakshak went into the office room?"

"No, Inspector sahib," Balram replied. "I saw Thakshak arrive earlier in the evening, around seven o'clock, I think, and then he had dinner with Judge sahib and madam. But I do not know when he went into the office room."

Inspector Anand made a mental note to ask Mrs. Pillai. "Go on."

"Mrs. Pillai yelled out: 'Thakshak! Open the door! What is going on in there? Why isn't Mohan saying anything?' But it was a good four to five minutes before I heard the bolts being drawn back inside, and the door opened. I rushed in and saw the Judge collapsed in his armchair behind his desk. Blood had seeped on to his kurta from a wound in his chest. I felt his pulse and could tell he was dead." Balram paused and tears glistened in his eyes. He swallowed and continued, "Madam screamed when she saw the sight, then collapsed into a chair, gasping and crying."

"What was Thakshak doing at the time?"

"Thakshak was pale and trembling and saying excitedly: 'Someone fired a shot through the window!'. At that point the watchman came to the office door. I shouted at him to immediately search the compound for intruders. I told madam that we should call the police. Since she was in a state of emotional collapse, I told her that I would do it, and called Police Headquarters."

"Why did you call police headquarters and not the local police station?" asked the Inspector.

Balram looked distressed and said, "Inspector sahib, forgive me, but I felt that a murder like this should be handled by the CID and not by our local station-wallas."

"You are right, of course, Balram," Inspector Anand said. "But not every driver knows that."

"I have been with the judge long enough to gain a knowledge of the inner workings of the police department, Inspector sahib. Also, I served as the judge's bodyguard and not just his driver."

The Inspector immediately pounced on that statement. "So Judge Pillai felt the need to have a bodyguard?"

"Judge sahib was telling me that from time to time he would get threats from unknown persons."

Inspector Anand felt his pulse quicken. This sounded promising. "How did those threats come? Via phone calls? Or letters?"

"Via phone calls. Judge sahib told me that he would occasionally get a threatening phone call."

"Did these calls make the judge afraid? Did he go about in fear for his life?"

"No, Inspector sahib." Balram shook his head. "He was a very brave man. He did not in the least have any fear. But at the same time, he felt that it was only prudent to employ a bodyguard, which is why I served as both driver and bodyguard."

Gazing at Balram Singh's tall figure with its unmistakable appearance of power and strength, Inspector Anand thought to himself that Judge Pillai could not have selected a better man to act as his bodyguard. But unfortunately it had not helped tonight.

"Have you had any prior training as a bodyguard, Balram?" he asked.

"Before coming to work for Judge Pillai, I served as a havildar in the Indian Army."

"What made you leave the Army and come to work for the judge?"

"My regiment was stationed here in Trivandrum, and our commanding officer told us that Judge sahib was looking for a bodyguard-cum-driver. The salary was good, and I was getting tired of being posted here and there, all over the country. I wanted to settle down, Inspector sahib, and I liked Trivandrum."

"I see. Now, getting back to the murder, did Thakshak explain why it took him so long to open the door?"

"He said that he was attending to Judge sahib. He said when the shot was fired through the window, it struck Judge sahib in the chest, knocking him back in his armchair. Thakshak said he was frozen with shock for some moments, then he ran to the bathroom, grabbed the towel that was hanging there, and tried to stem the flow of blood. He said he did this for a few minutes, but thinks Judge sahib was already dead by then."

"Did Thakshak see who fired the shot through the window?"

"He said he was facing Judge sahib and had his back to the window."

"Did he run to the window and try to see if he could catch a glimpse of the killer?"

Balram shook his head. "No. He said that he was so shocked by what had happened that his only thought was to administer to the judge."

"Did the watchman see anyone?"

"He said that he did not. But he is old, and his eyesight is not as good as it used to be."

Inspector Anand made some more notes in his notebook, then closed it and rose to his feet. "You have been very helpful, Balram. I will now go and talk to Mrs. Pillai and Thakshak."

"Very good, Inspector sahib."

Inspector Anand made his way back to the sitting room. Constable Varghese was standing obediently next to the double doorway that led into the house, staring gloomily at the garden.

The Inspector told him to take the flashlight from the police jeep and search the garden for signs of any intruder who might have been there, paying particular attention to the area under the window of the office room.

# Chapter 4

Inspector Anand decided that he would talk to Mrs. Pillai first, and obtain her statements, before questioning the nephew. He reasoned that the poor lady was dealing with a tremendous shock, was probably worn out, and would want to go and lie down. Moreover, since the nephew had actually been in the office room with the judge when the murder had taken place, questioning him would take longer and he did not want to keep Mrs. Pillai waiting that long.

Entering the sitting room, he said, "Mrs. Pillai, please accept my apologies, but I want to question you first, then Thakshak, as to what occurred here tonight."

"I cannot wait!" Thakshak said belligerently. "I have to get back to my hostel."

"This is a murder investigation," Inspector Anand told him grimly. "No one is allowed to leave until I say so."

"I will complain to your superiors!"

The Inspector had never allowed himself to be intimidated by a suspect, and he was not about to do so now. He said, "Go right ahead. But you have to stay here until I finish questioning you."

"Thakshak, you have to behave!" Mrs. Pillai said angrily. "Especially in light of what has happened here. We have to help the Inspector as much as we can so that he can catch whoever did this awful thing."

This unexpected support from Mrs. Pillai surprised the Inspector and he gave her a grateful glance.

"Would you like a glass of water, Inspector?" she asked. "Or a cup of tea, perhaps?"

Inspector Anand's estimate of the lady went up by several notches. She was considerate enough to think of his needs despite what she had just gone through.

"Not right now, thank you, Mrs. Pillai," he said. "Now, please tell me what happened tonight." Turning to Thakshak, he added, "I want you to stay quiet until I have finished talking to Mrs. Pillai. Then you will have your turn."

"I was sitting here after we had finished our dinner, reading a magazine," Mrs. Pillai began. "My husband had gone into his office room, accompanied by Thakshak."

"Did he ask Thakshak to go with him?"

"Yes, he said that he had something important to discuss."

"Mrs. Pillai, when did Thakshak arrive tonight?"

"He came around seven o'clock and had dinner with us."

"I see. Please go on."

"After they went into the office room, I heard my husband yelling at his nephew, and Thakshak yelling back. Both of them sounded very angry. Then I heard a sharp 'crack!' sound, and I heard my husband cry out."

"What time was that, Mrs. Pillai?"

She looked doubtful. "I am sorry, Inspector, but I was so involved in what I was reading that I did not pay much attention to the time."

"If you were to guess, around what time would you say you heard the sound of the gunshot?"

Mrs. Pillai frowned in concentration. "I would say, around 9:15 pm."

That tallied with the time Balram had given him, thought the Inspector. He made a quick entry in his notebook, and said, "Pray continue, madam."

"You can well imagine, I was very startled and scared. I immediately got up to go and see what was the matter. At the same time, Balram came rushing out of the kitchen and ran out of the front door to the veranda, and to the office room. I followed him as fast as I could. When I got there, I found Balram knocking hard on the office door, shouting 'What has happened? Judge sahib! Is everything allright?' I saw him trying to open the door, but it wouldn't open. It appeared to be bolted on the inside."

"Was that normal?" Inspector Anand asked. "Did the judge usually close and bolt the office door when he went in there?"

Mrs. Pillai shook her head emphatically. "No, Inspector, it was definitely most unusual. Mohan would retire to his office room after dinner on most nights, where he would sit and review case files, or just sit and read, and usually, he did not even close the office door, unless he had a visitor. But bolting it on the inside — never!"

"Uncle Mohan bolted the door himself!" Thakshak burst out.

Inspector Anand raised his left hand with his palm facing the young man. "Please be quiet. You will have your turn. Pray continue, Mrs. Pillai."

"I banged on the office door, and shouted to Thakshak to open it. But it was a good five minutes before we heard the bolts being drawn back and the door opened. Thakshak was pale and trembling and his breath was coming in gasps. Balram pushed him aside and ran inside, and I followed. And then I saw my husband, Inspector, just as you saw him now, slumped back in his chair, with blood on his kurta. Oh, it was awful!" Mrs. Pillai clasped her hands together and closed her eyes. Tears began to run down her cheeks.

Inspector Anand waited patiently till she regained control of herself and wiped her eyes with the edge of her sari. "It must have been very difficult for you," he said gently. "I do apologize, madam, for putting you through this, but you understand, I'm sure, that I have to get the facts as quickly as possible so that I can make progress towards solving the case."

"Don't worry, Inspector, I understand. You have to do your duty."

"Did Thakshak explain what happened and why it took him so long to open the door?"

"Thakshak said that someone fired a shot through the window, striking my husband in the chest. He said that he was so shocked that he could not move for several moments, and then when he saw the blood seeping out of Mohan's chest, he ran into the bathroom, grabbed a towel and tried to stem the flow of blood. He said that

that was why he did not open the door right away."

Thus far, Mrs. Pillai's evidence agreed with what Balram Singh had told him, thought Inspector Anand. Aloud, he said: "Mrs. Pillai, could you tell me more about Thakshak?"

"He is my husband's nephew, Inspector. Mohan had just one brother. The brother passed away last year, just as Thakshak was about to enter college. Thakshak's mother had passed away when he was young, so with the death of his father, the boy was left as an orphan. My husband said that he would pay for Thakshak's college education. Thakshak said that he could study better if he were to stay in the college hostel instead of living here, and my husband agreed to that also, but somewhat reluctantly."

Mrs. Pillai paused, glanced at Thakshak, and hesitated. It was clear that there was something more she wished to say, but not in his presence. Inspector Anand swiftly made up his mind that he would return the next day to talk to her privately.

"Balram said that your husband had received threatening calls...?" he began, but before he could go any further, Mrs. Pillai interrupted, eyes opened wide:

"Threatening calls? He never mentioned anything like that to me, Inspector! What threats?"

"Sorry, madam, I do not know the nature of the threats or what was said. All Balram said was that the judge had told him that from time to time he would receive threatening calls."

"This is the first time I have heard of this. But why would Mohan tell Balram about threatening phone calls and not me — his own wife?" demanded Mrs. Pillai.

Inspector Anand paused for a moment before replying. Then he said, gently, "Perhaps the Judge didn't tell you because he did not want you to worry. He would tell Balram because Balram is also his bodyguard."

Mrs. Pillai pondered this for a few minutes, then heaved a sigh and said, "You're right, Inspector. Mohan would not want me to worry."

They were interrupted by the sound of voices outside. The Inspector excused himself, stepped out onto the veranda and saw that the forensics team had arrived. He was glad to see that the team was headed up by Dr. Revathy, a no-nonsense medical examiner who was very good at her job.

"Hello, Dr. Revathy," he greeted her.

"Hello yourself. What do you mean by dragging me out at this hour?" she demanded in mock anger.

"A murder," the Inspector explained succinctly.

He could tell that Dr. Revathy was momentarily startled. "Really? In this nice neighborhood? Anyway, where's the victim? The sooner I get to work, the sooner I can go back home."

Inspector Anand led her and her team to the office room and the body. Leaving the forensics team to do their work, he returned to the sitting room and said, "Mrs. Pillai, your evidence has been most helpful. I'll call you or come here tomorrow if I have further questions, if you don't mind."

"Certainly, Inspector. I am now going to go upstairs to my bedroom and lie down. The events of this night have been very shocking, very hard to cope with."

"I can understand, madam. Please rest assured that I will make every effort to get to the bottom of this and find the criminal as quickly as possible."

She gave him a grateful look, rose to her feet, and made her way to the staircase at the far end of the sitting room.

# Chapter 5

Now it was finally the nephew's turn to be questioned. As events had turned out, this was the most important witness, one who had actually been on the spot where the murder had taken place. Recalling Thakshak's earlier outburst regarding the need to get back to his hostel, Inspector Anand pondered for a few moments about how best to approach this recalcitrant young man. Finally he said, "I don't want to keep you here any longer than necessary. So let's get right to the point: what were you and your uncle quarreling about, in the office room?"

"That was a private matter, and nothing to do with you," Thakshak responded rudely.

A spasm of anger swept through the Inspector. Impudent young pup! He glared at the hostile young man and said sharply, "Let me remind you once again, this is a murder investigation, and nothing can be considered private. Moreover, withholding information from a police officer is not only an unwise thing to do, but is also a punishable offense. Would you prefer that I haul you off to Police Headquarters, put you in the Interrogation Room, and question you there?"

The young man's belligerence was replaced by a look of genuine fear. He shrank back in his armchair, and said, sulkily, "My uncle was yelling at me that I was not paying attention to my studies and he was tired of spending all this money on my education. I got angry myself and started yelling back at him."

"And then what happened?"

"All of a sudden, I heard a sound like that of a car backfiring, and my uncle, who had been standing behind his desk, was knocked back into his armchair. I saw a red stain begin to spread across the front of his kurta. I stood in complete shock for maybe a minute, then I rushed to his side. I could see that there was a small round hole in the front of his kurta, and I realized that he had been shot. I dashed to the bathroom, grabbed the towel that was hanging there, and came back to my uncle and pressed the towel against his chest, hoping to stem the flow of blood. But, by that time, he was not breathing and I could tell that he had passed away."

"Did you not hear Balram Singh and your aunt banging on the office door and yelling to be let in?"

"Yes, I did, but I was too busy attending to my uncle to pay any attention to it right away. When I realized that my uncle was beyond help, I went to the door and unbolted it and let them in."

"Did you catch a glimpse of who fired the shot through the window?"

Thakshak shook his head. "I was facing my uncle and had my back to the window."

"So you did not go to the window and look outside to see if you could catch a glimpse of the assailant?"

"When the shot was fired, I was frozen with shock for about a minute. After that, my only thought was to attend to my uncle."

The young man's story sounded plausible. Inspector Anand said, "Very well, you can leave now. But first, give me the name of your college. And don't attempt to leave town or anything foolish like that. I might need to question you further."

Some of the young man's defiance returned. "You're trying to pin this on me, aren't you? I know you police-wallas. Pin the crime on someone on the spot, make an arrest, hold a press conference, and — case closed!"

"I am not here to 'pin' this crime on anyone, as you put it," said the Inspector, trying to control his anger. "My job is to find the killer, whoever it may be. Those who are innocent have nothing to fear. Now, kindly give me the name of your college."

Thakshak provided the Inspector with the information, then got to his feet and dashed out through the door, almost colliding with Dr. Revathy. He ran to his Vespa scooter, parked in the driveway behind his uncle's car, climbed on it, and kick-started it to sputtering life. He was shaking. Uppermost in his mind was the thought that he wanted to get away from this place as quickly as possible, back to his college hostel, amongst the comforting company of his friends. God, what an evening! It had been like a nightmare. He tried to erase the picture of his uncle, reeling back from the shot, from his mind. His poor uncle! That damn police inspector, looking at him as if he was a criminal! As he drove through the deserted streets towards his college campus, he thought gratefully of the half empty bottle of whiskey hidden in the cupboard of his room at the college hostel. He would take a good shot of it tonight, and try to sleep.

Dr. Revathy frowned after Thakshak's disappearing figure and asked, "Who was that?"

"The murdered man's nephew," Inspector Anand replied. "He was actually in the office room when the Judge was shot."

"Was he, indeed. Did he see anything?"

"He claims that the shot was fired through the window when he had his back to it, and did not see anyone."

"I would keep an eye on that young man, if I were you," Dr. Revathy said. "Anyway! I'm done. Bullet to the heart. Death must have been instantaneous. The bullet passed through the body and lodged in the armchair. I dug it out. Here it is," and she handed the Inspector a white envelope. "I figured you might need it as evidence."

"You think of everything," Inspector Anand said gratefully.

"Somebody has to," she retorted, smiling. "We're taking away the body. I'll do a post-mortem and send you the results in, let's see — two to three days?"

"Thank you, doctor," the Inspector said, but Dr. Revathy had already swung around and was going down the veranda steps, following the two men who were carrying away the sheet-covered body on a stretcher.

Constable Varghese, managing to look even more dour than before, came up the veranda steps from the garden, flashlight in hand.

"Did you spot anything?" Inspector Anand asked, hopefully.

"No, Inspector," Varghese shook his head. "I did not see any signs of an intruder having been here."

It's quite dark now, thought the Inspector, and it would be hard to spot signs of an intruder, even with a flashlight. He would come back tomorrow during the day and search the garden more thoroughly. He turned to Balram Singh, who was standing patiently on the veranda, and said, "I would like the office door locked now and the key given to me. Can you do that? I want to come back tomorrow and conduct a further examination of the room and I want it to be left undisturbed in the meantime."

"*Zaroor*, Inspector sahib." Balram went into the office room, and returned in less than a minute, turning off the lights, closed and locked

33

the heavy door, and handed the Inspector a large steel key.

"Is this the only key?"

"Yes, Inspector sahib."

"Thank you, Balram. I am done for tonight. Please let Mrs. Pillai know in the morning that I will be returning to examine the garden and the office room. Also, I may have further questions for her."

"I will do so, Inspector sahib."

"Where do you sleep, Balram? Do you have a residence somewhere close by?"

"I sleep here only," the tall Sikh replied. "There is a servant's quarters behind the kitchen, where we have been given a room with an attached bathroom. Judge sahib felt that as bodyguard, I should be here twenty-four hours."

"When you say 'we', Balram, you mean you and your wife?" Inspector Anand asked.

"That's correct, Inspector sahib," Balram said. "Actually, when I first came to work for Judge sahib over twenty years ago, I was young and unmarried. After a few years, my parents in my village in Punjab said that they had found a very nice girl for me to marry. When I told Judge sahib and madam about this, they very kindly gave me two weeks leave. I travelled to my village and got married and brought my bride back with me. Madam said that she could work in the house as the maid servant. Then madam taught her to cook Kerala dishes and she became the cook as well." Balram gave a rare smile and chuckle, and said, "My wife's Kerala cooking was terrible, at first! But madam was patient, and my wife soon picked it up, and became quite good at making southern dishes. Also, Judge sahib had a fondness for north Indian food as well, so he was delighted to have a cook who could make north Indian dishes like chicken tikka masala, choley and such."

A very nice arrangement, Inspector Anand thought. Husband and wife team, living on the premises.

On his way out, he decided to talk to the watchman who had opened the front gates. The old man was sitting on a wooden stool by the side of the front gate, dozing. Inspector Anand placed a hand on his shoulder and shook him awake. When the old watchman saw who it was, he stood up as erect as he could, and saluted. Most likely another old ex-army man, thought the Inspector.

"Did you hear the sound of a gunshot?" he asked.

"What, Inspector?" the old man cupped his hand behind his right ear.

"I asked, did you hear a gunshot?" the Inspector repeated the question, more loudly this time.

The watchman shook his head. "No, inspector. But then, I am hard of hearing."

"What were you doing tonight?"

"I was sitting here as usual on my stool, inspector."

"When did you notice something was wrong?"

"Oh!" said the old man. "I saw Balram pounding on the office door and yelling to be let inside."

"Was Mrs. Pillai there as well?"

"Yes, inspector. Memsahib came out of the sitting room and joined Balram in front of the office door. She also yelled to be let inside."

"And then what happened?" the Inspector asked.

"After some time — maybe five minutes, the office door was opened by the judge's nephew. Balram and memsahib rushed inside and I heard her scream."

"Then what did you do?"

"I went over to the door of the office room. Balram shouted at me to immediately search the entire compound for intruders. He looked very upset, Inspector, not at all like his usual self. I did what I was told, but did not see anyone. I came back and reported to Balram, and he then told me to resume my post by the front gate."

The Inspector thanked him, walked out through the big iron gates, and got into the police jeep with Constable Varghese. He told the driver, Constable Kurian, to drop him back home. He leaned back in his seat, extremely tired, as the police jeep sped back through the deserted streets.

After he was dropped off in front of his house, Inspector Anand unlatched the front gate and stood staring at the silent, empty bungalow. Where was the lovely wife he had come home to every day for more than thirty years? She was gone for ever. Memories of how she would greet him as he came home at the end of the day, always with a welcoming smile on her face, swept over him. Feeling old and depressed, he slowly walked up the path that led to his veranda, unlocked the front door and let himself into his dark, empty house.

# Chapter 6

Inspector Anand woke up late the next morning, at 9:30 am. Exhausted from the late activity of the previous night, he had slept through the early-morning musical clanging of the bells ringing out in the small temple at the end of the street, which usually served as his wake-up call.

He went into the kitchen and made himself a big mug of strong chai. Carrying the mug, he unlocked and unbolted his front door and went out onto his front veranda. The daily newspaper was lying there as usual, thrown there with unerring aim by the delivery man. The Inspector sat down in his wicker chair and while drinking his chai, quickly perused the newspaper. The main section was full of the usual political news and other events happening in India and around the world. There was no mention of the murder of Judge Mohan Pillai. That was not surprising, the Inspector reflected; the murder had occurred too late last night for today's edition. No doubt the news of the murder would leak out somehow. It would only be natural for Mrs. Pillai to inform the judge's relatives, her own relatives, and close friends, and the news would spread. Given the judge's prominence in the city, the newspaper was bound to put in a column about it, at the very least.

Inspector Anand finished reading the paper and sat gazing at his front garden and surrounding neighborhood. He never got tired of gazing at the beautiful greenery of Trivandrum, the sight of tall coconut palms swaying gently in the breeze, and banana trees with their big, broad leaves, that seemed to grow just about everywhere around town.

It was a bright, sunny day, typical for that time of year, with a brilliant blue sky overhead. On the narrow street running past his garden wall, people were going about their errands for the day. Some of those who knew the Inspector waved and called out a cheery "Good morning!" as they passed by and he waved back in reply. A vegetable seller was trundling his cart loaded with heaps of fresh tomatoes, potatoes, and squash down the street, calling out his prices. He came daily, and counted among his clientele many of the housewives in the neighborhood. A maid came out of one of the houses across the street, cloth bag in hand, and started inspecting the heaps of vegetables on his cart with suspicious eyes.

She poked at some of the tomatoes and complained of their poor quality. The vegetable seller angrily retorted that his tomatoes were excellent and freshly picked. He and the maid were old adversaries and skirmished daily, but she was also one of his most loyal customers.

Inspector Anand fell into a nostalgic reverie, thinking of his dear late wife. Even though almost two years had passed by since she died, it was still so hard for him to reconcile himself to her absence. Not a day went by, not one, when he did not miss her. He would never see her again in person, never be able to hold her hand in his, or talk to her. He reminisced about how they would frequently sit on the veranda together, idly chatting of whatever came to mind, or they would just sit in companionable silence, enjoying the sights and sounds coming from the street, feeling content and secure in the deep love they held for each other. He had treasured those moments, and had never imagined that they would end so prematurely, that the person he loved more than anyone else in the world would be taken from him while she was still in the prime of her life. He missed her lovely face, her wonderful smile, and kind nature. He missed the sound of her bustling about in the kitchen, and having their meals together. After her death, he felt that all joy had been sucked out of his life.

He was roused out of his reverie by the sound of his front gate being opened. It was his maid, Jyothi, a short, rotund, cheerful lady who came by once a day to clean his house and wash up the pots, pans and dishes in the kitchen sink. Jyothi had been hired by his wife over twenty years ago when she was just in her late teens, and had been their faithful maid ever since. His wife had always treated her well, with kindness, and as a result she had been devoted to his wife and had displayed almost as much anguish as the Inspector at her passing away.

Jyothi called out a cheerful greeting as she came up the driveway. She climbed up the short flight of steps leading to the front veranda and chatted with him for a few minutes, filling him in on the gossip around the neighborhood, before continuing on into interior of the bungalow to do her chores. She generally stayed for about an hour.

Inspector Anand usually stayed on the veranda or wandered around his garden while Jyothi performed her house cleaning, so as to not get in her way. He finished reading the newspaper, and then got up and went out to his garden, inspecting his plants, and watering the ones that appeared dry. Some of his vegetable plants hung heavy with ripe bounty; he would have to remember to take his gardening scissors, snip off the ripe vegetables and store them in his refrigerator, to be made into a nice curry when he had the chance.

The sun was beating down fiercely and it was becoming quite hot, so he headed back to the relative coolness of his veranda. Jyothi came out of the house, saying that she had completed her tasks. She asked the Inspector what time he was planning to go to work the next day, which was Monday, so that she could time her arrival and be done before he left for work. He told her that he was planning to leave for work early, so she needn't come tomorrow. Perhaps she could come the following day, which would be Tuesday, around 8:00 am?

After the maid left, Inspector Anand decided to head to his office at Police Headquarters; he had paperwork to catch up on, including filing the First Information Report and completing other documents on the murder case. He got to his feet, went inside, took a quick bath and changed into a comfortable short-sleeved shirt and slacks. He felt that there was no need to wear his uniform, since this particular Sunday was an official day off from work for him. In the past, he had always made it a point to spend his days off in his wife's company; but after her death, he never minded working on his days off when it was necessary.

He locked the front door and headed out to his car parked on the gravel driveway, an ancient 1939 Hanomag sedan. This was a German car his father had owned and had loved to tinker with on his days off. When his father passed away, Inspector Anand had been too young to have a driver's license, so one of his uncles had acquired it, and when that uncle had in turn died, the old car, lovingly maintained, had been bequeathed to Inspector Anand. Although the car was very old, he was loath to part with it; it felt like part of the family. Moreover, it was a very rare make; he had read that there were only a few of its kind around the world, and fewer still in India. Fortunately, he had found an excellent and honest mechanic who kept it running well.

On the way to Police Headquarters, Inspector Anand stopped for lunch at one of his favorite restaurants, not too far from his house. This restaurant was renown for the excellent quality of its vegetarian food. It attracted a loyal crowd, especially on Sundays; herds of families, couples with their children, grandparents, uncles and aunts, all talking at once. By sheer luck, he was able to secure a small table in one corner, where he could sit by himself. The restaurant owner, who knew that the Inspector's wife had passed away, came over to his table and briefly chatted with him, inquiring anxiously about his health and how the Inspector was carrying on.

The Inspector finished his lunch, and continued the drive to Police Headquarters. Arriving in his office, he completed the FIR and other necessary paperwork on the case and updated his case diary; he had always found it useful to do this as soon as possible at the beginning of a criminal investigation, while his memory was still fresh as to the events that had occurred. Fortunately for him, few of his colleagues appeared to be around, and he was able to concentrate on his work uninterrupted.

Inspector Anand then sat back and pondered his next move. Although Constable Varghese, acting under his instructions, had scoured the garden of Judge Pillai's residence last night with the aid of a flashlight, it had been dark and it was possible that he had missed a clue. The Inspector felt that he should return during daylight hours and re-examine the front garden thoroughly. He had noticed large oleander bushes lining the front garden wall; it was possible that an intruder could have hidden behind one of those bushes in the darkness of the night without being seen by the old night watchman, waiting for an opportune moment to fire a shot through the window at the judge. Perhaps an examination of these bushes during daylight would yield some evidence of a miscreant having been there the previous night.

It struck him at that point that the murderer must have been someone who was familiar with the judge's habit of retiring to his office room after dinner every night. Perhaps the fact that the judge's nephew Thakshak had also been in the room last night had appeared to the killer as a chance to pin suspicion on another person?

Inspector Anand felt that he also had to consider the possibility that Thakshak was lying, and there was in fact no mysterious assailant who had fired a shot through the window, and it was Thakshak himself who had shot the judge. After all, he and the judge had been heard having a violent quarrel before the shot was fired. But then, where had Thakshak got the gun to shoot the judge with? He had been dressed last night in just a short-sleeve shirt and slacks. It would have been difficult for him to hide a gun on his person; even a very small gun in his trouser pocket, or elsewhere, would have been noticed. Besides, the bullet did not look like one that had been fired from a small gun. Moreover, what would be Thakshak's motive? Judge Pillai was paying for his college education, so killing him would have been like killing the goose that laid the golden eggs.

But there remained the unavoidable fact that Thakshak had not opened the office door for a good four to five minutes after the shot was heard. Was the delay because he was administering to the judge, as he had said, or was it because he was trying to hide the murder weapon? Inspector Anand came to the conclusion that he needed to thoroughly search the judge's study.

Come to think of it, what about Balram? He had stated that he had been in the kitchen, eating his dinner, when the shot had been fired. But he could have slipped out of the kitchen through the back door, gone around to the front garden via the side of the house, then fired the fatal shot. Balram himself had stated that such a route was feasible. After all, it was his own wife who had been serving him dinner, and she would probably back up his story and provide him with a good alibi.

But no, thought Inspector Anand, that theory was absurd. Balram had been the Judge's faithful servant and bodyguard for over twenty years. Why would he suddenly want to murder him? He had displayed nothing but loyalty and affection for the Judge and his household when talking about them last night. Moreover, Mrs.

Pillai had stated that soon after she had heard the sound of the gunshot, Balram had come running out of the kitchen and into the living room, on his way to the veranda and the office room. So for now, at least, Balram would have to be eliminated as a suspect.

Inspector Anand left his office to drive to the Pillai residence. There was a great deal more traffic at that time of day; it seemed to the Inspector that traffic appeared to be getting worse and worse every year.

But that was probably true in every city in India, he reflected. The improving economy had resulted in more people being able to afford cars of their own, so there were now more and more cars on the streets, competing for space with ubiquitous auto rickshaws, buses, and taxis. Meanwhile, as always, pedestrians wandered recklessly all over the road, with a careless disregard for their own personal safety. The narrow streets, laid out decades ago, were crowded with buildings on both sides, and could not be widened to accommodate the increased amount of traffic.

When he brought his ancient Hanomag to a halt in front of the old two-storey house, he found a large young man, accompanied by a photographer, arguing with the old watchman, who was determinedly refusing to open the front gate. Seeing the Inspector pulling up in his car, the young man immediately made his way towards him, a notebook and pen at the ready.

"Inspector Anand!" the young man exclaimed. "This is a stroke of luck. You are just the man I wanted to see."

It was Raju Gopalan, a news reporter who the Inspector had encountered several times over the course of his career. Although he usually preferred to not talk to any reporters, feeling that such things were better left to his boss, the Deputy Superintendent of Police, there were times, such as now, when it simply could not be avoided. He was relieved that it was Raju who had been sent to cover the case, because he stuck to facts and did not quote people out of context or exaggerate what was said in an attempt to create a sensational story.

"What can you tell me about this murder, Inspector?" Raju asked, his pen poised over his already open notebook.

"What murder?" Inspector Anand asked, feigning surprise.

"Oh, come, come, Inspector, you can't fool me!" Raju shot back, grinning. "I heard that Judge Mohan Pillai had been shot last night - don't ask me how I found out; confidential sources and all that. You might as well tell me everything."

Inspector Anand provided him with the salient facts of the murder, with Raju scribbling it down in his notebook. However, he tactfully omitted the fact that the judge's nephew Thakshak had been in the room when the judge had been shot; the Inspector did not want Raju to go badgering the young man, and put a scare in him, till he had an opportunity to investigate him further.

"Do you have any suspects?" asked Raju.

"No one specific at this point. There are so many criminals around town who could have a grudge against Judge Pillai. Moreover, Raju, you have to remember that the murder took place just last night, so it's still in the very early stages of the investigation."

"Fair enough, Inspector," Raju said, closing his notebook. "Will you keep me informed if there are any developments?"

"Will do. And Raju, perhaps you can help me, too. You reporters hear a lot of gossip that goes on around town..."

"Me? Listen to gossip? Never!" Raju looked indignant, then broke into a smile and winked at the Inspector. "Just pulling your leg, sir. You were saying...?"

"If you hear of anyone who might have had a motive to commit this murder, will you let me know?"

"Of course. I will give you a call if I hear anything. Come on, let's go!" he called out to the photographer, who had been busy taking pictures of the judge's residence from the street.

# Chapter 7

After the reporter and photographer had left, the watchman unbolted the big iron gates and let Inspector Anand into the compound. Balram Singh was busy wiping down the judge's car with a rag and polishing the surface. He put his palms together, bowed, and said, "Namaste, Inspector sahib."

"Namaste, Balram. Would it be possible for me to speak to Mrs. Pillai?"

"Let me check. Madam might be taking her afternoon nap." He hurried off into the interior of the house, while the Inspector waited in the shade of the large veranda.

Balram returned a few minutes later, saying, "So sorry, Inspector sahib, but my wife informed me that madam has gone upstairs for her afternoon nap. Would you like to have my wife go and wake her?"

"No, please don't bother her. I wish to search the garden, and then the study. If Mrs. Pillai is awake by the time I leave, I will talk to her then."

Inspector Anand headed out to the front garden. Balram resumed what he had been doing earlier: cleaning and polishing the judge's car. The Inspector walked over to the area beneath the office room window. The front lawn ran all the way to the outer wall of the office room, where it jutted out into the front garden. There were no discernible footprints in the firm dry turf. He peered through the heavy iron bars running up and down the window; from that vantage point, the judge's desk and the armchair behind it were clearly visible. So, in theory, it looked like it would have been easy enough for a person standing there to have fired a shot through the window and hit the judge.

Inspector Anand walked across the lawn to the big oleander bushes next to the garden wall fronting the street, and looked through the bushes carefully. There was sufficient room between the bushes and the garden wall for someone to have hidden there, out of sight of the old watchman, especially at night. There was a profusion of dried leaves and broken twigs accumulated at the base of the oleander bushes. They appeared to be undisturbed. Taking one of the long twigs lying on the ground, the Inspector sifted through the dried leaves to see if a gun had been dropped or hidden there, but found nothing.

But what about the backyard behind the house? Could a miscreant have scaled the rear wall of the compound, and made his way along the side of the house to the front? Balram, when giving evidence the previous night, had said that such a route was feasible.

Inspector Anand made his way through the front garden to the left-hand side of the house, and discovered a four-foot gap between the side of the house and the compound wall, forming a narrow passage that presumably led to the backyard. The passageway, covered with gravel, appeared to be about forty feet in length. He walked down the passage towards the rear of the house. When he rounded the corner at the back end, he saw that he was in another shorter

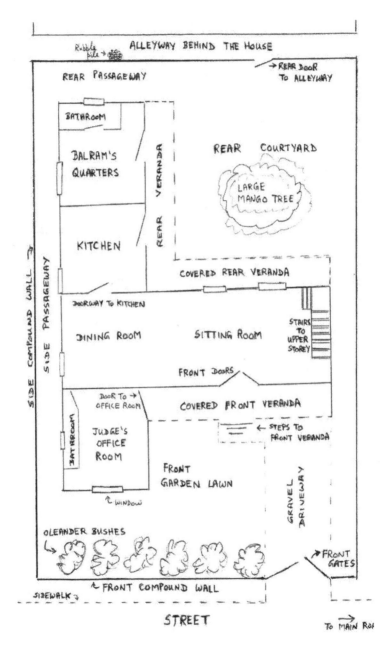

passage between the house and the what was now the rear wall of the compound. This passage was about ten feet long, and opened up into a large courtyard dominated by a huge mango tree.

By then, the Inspector was sweating profusely in the hot, muggy afternoon, and his shirt had become damp and was sticking to his back. He walked under the welcoming shade of the mango tree, and mopped his face with his handkerchief.

A tall lady dressed in a pink salwar-kameez and balancing a wicker tray of uncooked white rice against her left hip, came out of the doorway of one of the rooms, and called out sharply from the veranda: "*Hoi*, mister! What do you want here? Who are you?"

Inspector Anand realized that since he was dressed in plainclothes and not in his uniform, she could not be know that he was a police officer. He walked over to her and introduced himself.

Her face lit up with a warm smile. "Oh! Inspector, Balram told me about you. I am his wife, Kamal." She was slim and pretty, with dark eyes and an expressive face.

He explained that he was planning to search along the rear wall to see if there were any signs of someone having climbed over the back wall and into the compound the previous night.

Kamal clicked her tongue sympathetically. "It must be so hard for you police wallas, *na*, to go running around in this hot weather, looking for clues. I am sure your wife must quite worried."

She did not expect the change that came over the Inspector's face at her last words. It seemed to her that all light and life left his face in an instant, to be replaced by an infinite sadness. His shoulders slumped, and in a voice coated in grief, he said, "My dear wife is no more. She passed away about two years ago."

Kamal gasped and her eyes filled with tears. "Oh, Inspector ji, I am so sorry for your loss! It must be so hard for you. Please forgive me for reminding you of your wife, I didn't know..." She stopped falteringly.

"It's all right, Kamal ji, I think of her often, anyway" The Inspector said, managing to summon up a faint smile. "You did not know that she was no more, since it did not come up in my conversations with Balram. Pray think nothing of it."

She wiped the tears from her eyes, and said, "Please wait a minute, let me get you something cold to drink." She wheeled around and disappeared into the room behind. Judging from the appetizing smells emerging through the open doorway and window, Inspector Anand guessed that this was in all likelihood the kitchen. Kamal reappeared a few minutes later, carrying a tall glass containing what appeared to be cold lemonade. Little drops of condensation were forming on the outside of the glass.

The Inspector took the proffered glass gratefully and took a big swallow. "Delicious! Thank you very much, this is just what I need."

"I make the nimbu-pani myself," said Kamal proudly. "Judge sahib used to love my nimbu-pani." Then her face fell and she sighed. "What a dreadful thing to happen, judge sahib shot just like that! I hope you catch the *badmash* who did this, Inspector sahib."

"I am certainly going to try my best," the Inspector said, finishing the lemonade and handing the glass back to her. "Kamal ji, did you happen to notice anything suspicious in the backyard last night?"

Kamal shook her head. "No, I was busy cooking dinner for the family from afternoon on, and then serving them in the dining room later in the evening. After the family had eaten, I cleared up the dining table, and brought the remaining food back to the kitchen. I called Balram, who was out front, to come and have his dinner, and then I was busy serving him and cleaning up the kitchen. But when he was halfway through his meal, we heard a loud 'crack!' sound coming from the front of the house and heard the judge cry out. Balram immediately jumped to his feet, washed his hands quickly, and ran off."

What she had just said tallied with what Balram had told him last night. Smiling at her, Inspector Anand said, "Thank you, your lemonade was most refreshing. But I should resume my investigation, and search the area around the back wall." He nodded politely, turned around and made his way there. Kamal gazed pensively after his tall, lanky figure striding away for a few moments, then sighed deeply and returned to the interior of the kitchen.

As he made his way towards the rear of the large backyard, the Inspector noticed a battered wooden door set into the rear wall. It was shut, and heavy iron bolts kept it closed. He drew back the bolts, opened the heavy door, which squealed protestingly on its rusty hinges, and stepped outside. He found himself in a narrow alleyway, overgrown with weeds, that ran along the rear of the houses.

His face grew thoughtful. It would have been very feasible for someone to sneak into this alley, climb over the rear wall, and gain entry into the backyard of Judge Mohan Pillai's residence. As a matter of fact, there was a pile of concrete rubble about ten yards away, next to the rear wall, probably left over from some prior construction project. The Inspector walked over to the rubble pile, and climbed up to the top, using the wall for support. From that vantage point, he found that he could look over the top of the rear wall and into the backyard. A moderately athletic person standing on that pile would find it easy enough to hoist himself over the wall after ensuring that the coast was clear. This mode of entry into the compound would be much more preferable to any miscreant who did not wish to be seen, as it was infinitely less risky than climbing over the front wall that faced the street. However, that also meant that the intruder would have to be knowledgeable enough about the neighbourhood to be aware of this narrow back alley. But that knowledge could be easily acquired; anyone who prowled around the neighbourhood for a few days could discover this back alley.

Inspector Anand stepped down from the concrete rubble pile, dislodging a few small pieces in the process. He examined the area around the pile and next to the wall carefully. The mud there was baked hard by the hot sun and displayed no footprints. He made his way down the alleyway, away from the judge's residence, scanning the ground as he did so. He was suddenly startled by a large black cat that sprang out of the tall weeds and bolted down the alley. Recovering himself, he almost laughed. An ill omen? The way this case was going, it seemed appropriate.

He made his way back to the battered wooden door that led to the backyard of the Pillai residence, closing and bolting it behind him. A rectangular area bordering the rear wall was planted with a vegetable garden. The plants and moist soil looked undisturbed. The remaining area around the base of the rear wall was weed infested and it was hard to tell if anyone had been there the previous night.

With the hot afternoon sun beating down on him, the Inspector found himself perspiring heavily again. He decided to move his quest indoors, into the judge's study, which he had planned to search, anyway. He walked around the side of the house to the front, and saw Balram standing in the shade of the veranda, no doubt taking a break from the afternoon heat. The Inspector climbed up the short flight of steps and joined him.

"Balram, I want to verify a point with you," he said. "From what I've gathered, after Judge Pillai and his family have eaten their dinner, your wife Kamal clears the dining table, takes the remaining food back into the kitchen, and then calls you to come and have your evening meal?"

"That's correct, Inspector sahib."

"What does the judge normally do during that time — while you're eating?"

"He would go to the office room, where he would work on some files, or sit and read."

"Would he be alone during that time?"

"Yes, unless he had a visitor."

"What kind of visitor would that be, Balram?"

"Usually a friend or colleague, Inspector sahib."

"Someone he was familiar with?"

"Yes."

"What if it was someone he did not know? Would he receive that person in his office room, anyway, while you were eating?"

"Yes."

"After you finished your meal, what would you normally do?"

"I would sit on the veranda, or stand near the front gates, chatting with the watchman, till Judge sahib left the office room and entered the house. Then I would lock up the office room and retire to my quarters."

"How long do you usually take to finish eating your dinner?"

"About half an hour."

"So, for about half an hour, the judge would be alone and unprotected in the office room?"

A look of distress appeared on Balram's face. "Yes, that is correct, Inspector sahib. But the judge and I had always felt that the risk to him was really during the time when he was being driven to his office, or around town. Judge sahib always thought that he was safe in his own house, behind the walls of the compound."

Trivandrum on the whole being a peaceful town, that was probably true, reflected Inspector Anand. Aloud, he said: "Please don't think that I am criticizing the security arrangements, Balram. After all, you have to have to eat at some point during the evening. What I'm trying to establish is that if some miscreant who wished to do the judge harm was somehow aware of the nightly routine, he would know that the half hour when you were in the kitchen would be an opportune time to sneak into the front garden and do what he wished."

The look of distress on Balram's face deepened. "Yes, that is true, Inspector sahib." Then he spread his hands wide. "But this has been Judge sahib's routine for many years. Why was he shot last night, and not before?"

The Inspector abruptly realized that Balram had made an excellent point. Why in particular had the murder taken place last night and not at some other time? He thought hard. Perhaps some new criminal case had come up before the judge, or was scheduled to come up, a case so damaging to the accused that the judge had to be silenced. The best way to find out would be to review the judge's recent cases, and cases scheduled to be presented in his court.

Meanwhile, since he was on the premises, he might as well search the office room, as he had planned. Thanking Balram, the Inspector made his way to the office room, unlocking the door with the key he had been given the previous night. The coolness of the room was a welcome relief after the heat and humidity outside. There was enough light coming in through the wide window that looked out onto the front garden to enable the Inspector to see the interior clearly.

Now, if Thakshak had shot the judge and then hurriedly hidden the gun somewhere in that room, where would he have hidden it? Inspector Anand gazed thoughtfully at the tall wooden bookshelves lining the wall. Typical of most bookshelves, there was a gap between the rows of books on each shelf and the back panel. It would have been easy enough for Thakshak to pull out one or two of the heavy volumes, hide the gun in the space between the books and the back panel, and replace the books. Anyone staring at the rows of hardbound books from the front would not be able to see a gun hidden behind.

Beginning with the bookshelf closest to the entry doorway, the Inspector began to methodically pull out the hardbound volumes, and check the space behind. While many of the volumes were devoted to law, he noted with pleasure that two shelves contained works of fiction by classical authors, both Indian and foreign: Rabrindanath Tagore, R.K. Narayan, Sarojini Naidu, V.S. Naipaul, Charles Dickens, Alexander Dumas, Mark Twain, and others. The judge was evidently a well-read man. It took him about an hour to search through all the bookshelves. Aside from a few odds and ends, such as paper clips and pens covered with a layer of dust, he found nothing.

He then began to look through the drawers of the judge's heavy wooden desk. The top shallow drawer held an assortment of pens, pencils, and notepads. The drawer on the right was deep and contained hanging manila folders, each one neatly labeled: taxes, insurance, household expenses, and so on. A folder labeled "Death threats" caught his attention. Inside it were two sheets of ruled paper, neatly inscribed with dates, time of day, and a brief sentence or two: "Unknown person called and said I would die soon", "Unknown person called and threatened to kill me," and so on. The judge had been a methodical, organized man. There were thirteen such entries on the two sheets of paper. The dates began some fifteen years ago.

The sheet of paper with the death threats noted on it gave credence to what he had said to reporter Raju Gopalan earlier, that given the judge's hard-line stance towards the criminal class, there were bound to be many reprehensible individuals who might have wanted to kill the judge. The Inspector reflected gloomily that he might end up having to scour the entire underworld of Trivandrum in search of the killer. It was going to be akin to searching for the proverbial needle in the haystack.

The Inspector pondered his next move. He might as well see if Mrs. Pillai had woken up from her afternoon nap and talk to her. He replaced the file, closed the drawer, and left the office room, closing and locking the door behind him. The double doors that provided entry into the sitting room stood open, and he was glad to see Mrs. Pillai seated on the sofa, drinking a cup of tea. She looked very tired, and her face bore signs of the strain from the events of the previous night. Catching sight of him, she said: "Ah, Inspector, so you are back?   Any progress in the case?"

"Not much, madam, I am sorry to say," Inspector Anand replied, ruefully.   "I searched your front garden and your backyard, to see if I could find any signs of an intruder.  But although I couldn't find any direct signs, that doesn't mean that some miscreant hadn't entered the compound last night.  We've not had any rain in some time, so the ground is hard, and there aren't any footprints.  Signs such as flattened grass, broken twigs and such, might have been caused by an intruder, but then again could be attributed to your gardener and others such as your watchman and Balram, going around their normal duties."

Mrs. Pillai heaved a heavy sigh and said, "It's not easy for you, is it, Inspector?"

"No, this case is quite a challenge," the Inspector agreed.  "But I want to assure you that I am going to do my best to find out who perpetrated this crime.  It doesn't do the forces of law and order any good if the murder of a law-abiding, honest judge is allowed to go unresolved. I am going to review the judge's recent cases to see if I can find a motive.  That will take some time. Meanwhile, I would like to talk to you more about Thakshak.   I sensed yesterday that there was something more you wished to tell me, but not in his presence."

"That was very observant of you, Inspector," Mrs. Pillai said.  "But first, why don't you sit down? Would you like a cup of tea? Or something cold to drink?

"No thank you, madam. Kamal served me a glass of cold lemonade while I was searching the rear of the compound."

"Yes, she's a treasure, and so is Balram. I am so glad that they are both here to provide me with company and comfort during this very difficult time."

Mrs. Pillai waited until he had seated himself in the armchair with its back to the staircase, and began: "As I said last night, my husband Mohan had just one brother, and Thakshak is his son and only child. You probably recall that his mother had passed away when he was quite young, and his father raised him. Then his father passed away unexpectedly last year. At the time, Thakshak was in his 2nd year of college. Mohan found out that his brother had left very little money. He told Thakshak that he would pay for the rest of his college education, so that he could get a decent start in life."

She paused to drink some more of her chai, and continued: "Unfortunately, what happened was that Thakshak did not pay attention to his studies. Various people around town told us that he frequented gambling dens and drank heavily. You see, Inspector, the problem was that the boy had been thoroughly spoilt by his father, because his mother had died when he was very young. My brother-in-law was always very busy with his work, and did not pay sufficient attention to the boy. Thakshak did whatever he wanted to when he was growing up. When my husband heard about Thakshak's gambling and drinking, he was naturally very upset. He was going to tell Thakshak last evening that either he straighten out or else he would cut off all funds to him, not give him a paisa more."

That explained the after dinner fight between Judge Pillai and his nephew, Inspector Anand thought. But was that sufficient motive for Thakshak to shoot his uncle?

He saw that Mrs. Pillai was observing him shrewdly. She said, as though she had read his mind, "So you're thinking, Inspector, that Thakshak might have killed my husband?"

Inspector Anand spread his hands wide. "To be frank, madam, based on what you have told me, and also how long he took to open the door of the office room last night, he is definitely a suspect. But there are two big points in his favor. The first one is this: based on the way he was dressed, it appears very unlikely that Thakshak had a gun on his person when he arrived for dinner last night."

Mrs. Pillai nodded vigorously. "Yes, I assure you, Inspector, that Thakshak could not have had a gun concealed in his clothes when he came here last night. I am quite observant, you know, and I would have noticed it immediately. Guns are not small things."

"So, if he did not have a gun with him, how could he have shot the judge? The second point is that since it was the judge who was paying for his college education, why would Thakshak want to kill him?"

Mrs. Pillai pounced on this point eagerly. "Yes, it would be most foolish on his part to kill Mohan. While Thakshak has given indications of being a wild young man, I do not think that even he would go that far."

# Chapter 8

The next day being Monday, Inspector Anand woke up early and after drinking his morning tea, reading the newspaper, and getting ready, drove to his office. The Deputy Superintendent of Police would want to be updated on the progress of the case. The murder of Judge Pillai had appeared in the newspaper that morning, and there was little doubt that political pressure would already be mounting on the DSP to quickly solve the crime.

Therefore, it was not altogether surprising that, soon after he had settled himself behind the desk in his office and started on some of his reports, his phone rang and the voice of DSP Krishnan Nair asked him to come up to his office "right away".

Seated in one of the chairs facing the DSP's immense desk, Inspector Anand crisply summarized the salient features of the case. DSP Nair, a large man with a luxuriant mustache and thick graying hair, listened attentively, and when the Inspector had finished, said:

"Do you accept the nephew's story? That someone fired a shot through the window? Isn't it suspicious that the nephew — what's his name, Thakshak? — took so long to open the office room door?"

"Well, sir, the problem is this," said Inspector Anand. "If we assume that he shot the judge, where did he get the gun? He seems to have just come to eat dinner with his uncle and his wife, as he often did, and his attire — a short-sleeve shirt and slacks — appears to rule out the possibility of a gun on his person. The bullet retrieved from the body indicates that it was fired from a regular-sized revolver, not a tiny one. It would have been hard for Thakshak to hide a regular sized gun on his person without it being noticed. Mrs. Pillai assured me yesterday that if Thakshak had been carrying such a gun in his trouser pocket, or elsewhere on his person, she surely would have noticed it. As for the delay in opening the door, the nephew explained that it was because he was administering to his uncle, trying to stem the flow of blood and so on. That certainly seems plausible. There was a blood-soaked towel on the floor near the body of the deceased, which supports his story."

The DSP heaved a heavy sigh.

"If some *badmash* fired a shot through the window, killing the judge, you have a wide field of suspects to choose from," he said, gloomily. "Judge Pillai was a tough man who showed no leniency towards the criminals who appeared before him in court. He was also, by all accounts, a very honest man who could not be bribed or influenced in any way. Such a person would be a thorn in the side of the criminal element in town."

"That's what I thought too, sir," Inspector Anand said.

"Perhaps your best bet will be to conduct exhaustive inquiries to see if any suspicious looking character was seen hanging around in the vicinity of the judge's residence that evening. Also, keep your ear to the ground, and ask our constables to do the same. Some gang leader or thug might brag about having killed the judge. I will call the police stations around town and ask them to immediately notify us if they hear anything.  Let's hope we get a lucky break."

"Yes, sir."

"Let me not detain you any further, Inspector, so you can get on with it.  I need hardly tell you that the Chief Minister's office itself has already called me about this case.  Make this your number one priority.  Any other cases that you are working on can wait."

"Yes, sir.  I understand, sir."

"By the way, I have informed the Station House Officer in charge of the local police station with jurisdiction over that area, that we will be handling the case.  He was only too glad.  Can't blame him, really.  The local police stations are understaffed and have their hands full dealing with traffic accidents, petty crimes, strikes, and so forth."

Back in his office, Inspector Anand hurriedly updated his reports, and then made his way to the headquarters' canteen to fortify himself with a cup of tea before venturing out to resume his investigation.  Some five minutes later, he was sitting at one of the metal tables in the canteen, sipping a cup of steaming chai, and pondering on the case, when he received a hearty slap on his back, between the shoulder blades, causing him to spill a considerable portion of his tea onto the table.  He raised a wrathful face and saw that it was Inspector Bhaskaran, a large, boisterous individual and notorious back-slapper.

"Really, Bhaskaran!  Look at what you've done!  I've spilt most of my tea."

"I'll get you another chai," Bhaskaran said, laughing heartily. "I need one myself." He went to the counter, and returned a few minutes later, carrying two cups of steaming chai.

"I heard that you are handling the Judge Pillai murder," Bhaskaran said, easing his considerable bulk into a metal chair across the table. "What progress have you made thus far?"

Inspector Anand quickly brought him up to date.

"I'm glad that you're in charge of the case and not me," Bhaskaran said, with feeling. "It promises to be a real stinker. But I think I may be able to throw a suspect in your lap. Ever heard of Constable Rajakkan?"

Inspector Anand shook his head. "No, not that I recall."

"The events I am about to relate happened about eleven years ago. Rajakkan was a hard working constable, well thought of, posted at the Fort Police Station, and not here at headquarters, which could be why you haven't heard of him. I was posted at Fort Police Station myself before being promoted and transferred here to HQ, which is how I know about Rajakkan. He was married and had one daughter, whom he doted on. She meant everything to him. She was a good student, and there was every expectation that she would get into a good college, earn a degree and make a good life for herself. But then, suddenly, tragedy struck. When the girl was about 15 years old, she was diagnosed with cancer. I believe it was leukemia."

Bhaskaran paused to drink some of his tea, then continued. "Poor Rajakkan was absolutely distraught. I remember the day he told his colleagues. He was sobbing like a child. Then he pulled himself together and started taking his daughter to the best doctors in town. But treatment for cancer was terribly expensive back then, and he soon used up all the savings he had set aside for her college education."

"What did he do, then?" Inspector Anand asked, with a sense of foreboding.

"Rajakkan completely fell apart. He started taking bribes left and right to get money for his daughter's treatments. He threatened shopkeepers and took money from them. He took money from motorists that he had stopped for traffic violations. It was all very sad, really, because up until then he had been an honest, hardworking policeman without a stain on his record. But then, he was desperate and willing to do anything to help his daughter recover."

Bhaskaran paused and eyed Inspector Anand sadly. "Eventually, it all blew up, of course. Complaints began pouring in about him, and he was caught red-handed. He came up for sentencing in front of your Judge Mohan Pillai. The defense lawyer did his best. He pleaded for leniency, pointed out Rajakkan's prior honesty and hard work, how his daughter's condition had made him act the way he did, etc. But Judge Pillai was inflexible. He yelled at the wretched Rajakkan in court, saying he had betrayed the trust imposed on him by the police force, and sentenced him to ten years in jail."

"Now the story gets even more tragic," Bhaskaran continued. "While he was in prison, his beloved daughter died. I think that after her father was sentenced, she just lost the will to live.

I can only imagine what Rajakkan must have felt when he got the news. I would not be surprised if he blamed Judge Pillai for his daughter's death."

"Is Rajakkan out of prison?" Inspector Anand asked sharply.

"I heard that he had served his ten years of jail time and was released just a week ago." Bhaskaran leaned back in his chair and puffed out his cheeks. "So there you have it, Ashok: your number one suspect."

# Chapter 9

Inspector Anand gulped down the rest of his tea and hurried back to his office. It was clear to him that he needed to find the whereabouts of Rajakkan as quickly as possible, and question the man. How best to find out where this prime suspect was to be found? Seating himself in his chair, he called the Central Prison, and after being frustratingly transferred several times to different departments, he found himself speaking to the Head Clerk, who looked up his records and verified that yes, Rajakkan had indeed been released a week ago.

"Did he provide you with an address where he could be located?" asked the Inspector.

"You should talk to the Welfare Officer, Mrs. Vijayam," the Head Clerk said. "She is responsible for the pre-release programs for all prisoners. She also has to maintain case records for every prisoner."

"Do you have her phone number?"

"Yes, Inspector. Here it is." He read out the number to the Inspector, who jotted it down on his notepad. He thanked the Head Clerk for his assistance, and dialed the number he had been provided. After a couple of rings, a bright young female voice answered: "Welfare Officer's office, Central Prison."

"May I speak to the Welfare Officer Mrs. Vijayam?"

"Who is calling?"

"This is Inspector Ashok Anand with the Trivandrum Police CID."

"Oh! Inspector, please wait. I will see if Mrs. Vijayam is free."

After a wait of a few minutes, a gruff female voice came on the line and said: "Inspector Anand? This is Welfare Officer Mrs. Vijayam speaking."

"Madam, I am attempting to obtain information on the whereabouts of one Rajakkan, who was a prisoner there, and was released a week ago."

"Ah, yes, I remember him well. What would you like to know?"

"When he was released, did he provide an address where he could be located?"

"I'll have to look in my files. Please hold on for a few minutes, Inspector."

"Certainly, madam."

Inspector Anand heard the sound of a chair being pushed back, and metal filing cabinets being opened and closed. The Welfare Officer came back on the line and said: "This is the address Rajakkan provided when he left the prison," and read it out.

"Is Rajakkan some sort of trouble, Inspector?" she asked.

"He might be, madam, but at this point I am not sure," Inspector Anand replied truthfully. "I need to talk to him, in connection with an investigation. Can you tell me, what kind of prisoner was he?"

"In the beginning, when he first came to the prison, he was a very angry man. He would rave and rant about the judge who had sentenced him, and utter dire threats. Then, when he received the news that his daughter had died, he collapsed entirely. He would sit in a corner and cry all the time, refusing to eat. All life seemed to have gone out of him. I felt sorry for him, actually. It's very hard to lose a child. The other prisoners were kind to him, and tried to help him as much as they could."

The Welfare Officer paused, and then continued: "But then gradually, his bitterness returned. He blamed the judge for the death of his daughter, and he was heard saying that when he got out of prison, he would seek revenge. I tried my best to convince him not to harbor such dangerous thoughts, that his best course of action after his sentence was up was to work hard at whatever job he could get, and rebuild his life."

Inspector Anand thanked her, and hung up. He hurried out of his office, into the courtyard, and made his way to where the police vehicles were parked. He commandeered a police jeep and gave the driver the address he had obtained from the Welfare Officer at the Central Prison. Half an hours' driving brought them to a poorer section of town. As the police jeep wove its way through the narrow streets, the driver honking at pedestrians, stray dogs, goats, and chickens wandering about, a band of young street urchins ran behind them excitedly, calling out "Police! Police!" while other residents eyed the vehicle curiously as it went by. As was typical in that section of town, with its maze of narrow streets and alleyways and few, if any, street signs, they located the address only after numerous inquiries. The driver eventually pulled up in front of a small dilapidated row house.

Inspector Anand jumped out of the police jeep, climbed up the short flight of steps to the front veranda, and knocked on the weather beaten front door. After a few minutes, the door was opened, revealing a thin, faded woman who appeared to be in her mid thirties. At the sight of the Inspector in his uniform, she gasped audibly and her hand flew to her mouth.

"What do you want?" she asked faintly.

"Does Rajakkan live here?" asked the Inspector.

She hesitated, and observing the hesitation, Inspector Anand said sharply, "Please don't try to lie to me. Is he here?"

Tears filled her eyes. "Yes, but he is very sick."

"I see. Nonetheless, I wish to see him."

She nodded and turned around and led the way into the dingy interior. It took a few moments for the Inspector's eyes to get accustomed to the semidarkness inside, and then he saw a frail, thin man wearing tattered, threadbare clothes lying on his side on a cot in one corner of the room. His eyes were closed, his breath uneven, and spittle covered his lips.

"This is Rajakkan?" asked the Inspector.

"Yes."

"How long has he been like this?"

"Ever since he came home a week ago," the woman replied. Her voice broke and she started weeping silently.

"Has he seen a doctor?"

She shook her head, wiping the tears from her face with the edge of her shabby sari. "We cannot afford a doctor."

"Has he been out of the house at all?"

"No. He has just been lying here all the time."

Inspector Anand thought rapidly. It was clear that Rajakkan could not have committed the murder of Judge Mohan Pillai: the frail, sick man lying on the cot in that dark room had not even the strength to get up out of bed. He said: "Madam, Rajakkan needs medical care right away. I am going to send for an ambulance to take him to the nearest hospital. Are you his wife?"

She nodded. "Yes."

"Then please wait here while I call for an ambulance."

Inspector Anand stepped out of the house, and was surprised to find that a small crowd had gathered around the police jeep parked in the street. A big, brawny man sporting a ferocious mustache stepped forward and addressed the Inspector. He smelt strongly of alcohol and his eyes were bloodshot. "What are you doing to Rajakkan?" he demanded. "Are you taking him back to prison?"

Inspector Anand took stock of the situation. Long experience had taught him the dynamics of confrontation with a rebellious crowd. Telling the big man in front of him to mind his own business would probably just provoke the throng, and then who knew what would happen? No point into getting into a fight with these people, most of whom were probably neighbors and were acting out of genuine concern for Rajakkan, combined with a deep-rooted distrust of the police. So he said calmly, but loudly enough for the crowd to hear, "No, I am not taking him back to prison. He has already served his sentence. But he is very ill, and needs immediate medical attention. I am going to call for an ambulance to take him to the hospital."

The Inspector noted with satisfaction the effect his words had on the people gathered around. Belligerent looks faded from most of the faces, and they looked at each other uncertainly. But his words did not seem to appease the big man, who continued to glare at him. "Why should I believe you?" he demanded.

"If you wait here for another thirty minutes, you will see the ambulance pull up," retorted Inspector Anand.

An old lady hobbled out of the crowd, using her cane for support. She was a tiny woman, not more than five feet in height, with a small bird-like face alive with intelligence. Despite her diminutive size, it was evident that she commanded the respect of the people gathered around.

"Mayavi, you leave the police officer alone!" she cried. "He is a good man, I can tell. Let him help poor Rajakkan!" There were murmurs of agreement from the throng.

Sullenly, Mayavi stepped aside, allowing the Inspector to go over to the police jeep. He called police headquarters over the two-way radio, requesting an ambulance to be sent over, giving them the address.

# Chapter 10

After seeing the sick Rajakkan safely off to the hospital in an ambulance, Inspector Anand asked the police jeep driver to take him back to Police Headquarters. He felt despondent. Rajakkan now had to be eliminated as a suspect, and he was back to square one. He seemed to be making no headway in this case. His thoughts once again returned to the judge's nephew Thakshak. He could not rid himself of the feeling that the young man had not been entirely truthful, that he was trying to hide something.

Inspector Anand made up his mind. He would drive over to Thakshak's college campus and make some discreet inquiries about that young man. He had found in his experience that even casual inquiries regarding a suspect in his or her home ground frequently yielded surprisingly useful results. But first, he would go home from Police Headquarters, and change out of his uniform into plain clothes. It would be easier to make inquiries about Thakshak if he did not appear on the college campus in his police officer's uniform.

Arriving at the campus, he parked his car and sat in it, thinking. Instead of just wandering around, hoping to run into someone who knew Thakshak well, was there a central place he could go to, where students congregated and chatted freely, a place where they would be more inclined to gossip?

Ah, yes, of course: the college canteen. Having studied at a college himself, he knew that the canteen was usually the favorite spot for students to sit and gossip, a place where heated discussions and banter take place over endless cups of tea and snacks.

Inspector Anand got out of his car, and after a few inquiries, he was able to locate the large one-story building that housed the canteen. Entering it, he found a spacious hall filled with square metal tables with folding chairs arranged around each table. A long counter ran along the farther end of the hall, and behind it an assortment of cooks and servers were busy preparing food and serving students. Two old cash registers stood at one end of the counter. The smell of fried food and spiced tea hung heavy over the entire hall.

The Inspector glanced at his watch. It was not yet lunchtime, and the place was relatively empty. Only a few of the tables were occupied by students with plates of samosas, vadas, and other snacks in front of them, accompanied by steaming cups of chai or a bottle of cold soda.

He went up to one of the cash registers, and placed an order for two vadas and a cup of chai. After paying for his order (the cost was surprisingly reasonable, which, he reflected, was typical of most college canteens in India), he carried his plate and chai to an empty small table in the middle of the hall and sat down. The vadas were big and crispy on the outside, and a bite confirmed that they tasted as delicious as they looked. The accompanying coconut chutney was equally tasty.

After fifteen minutes, students started to wander in, and after half an hour, the place started getting filled up.

"Excuse me, uncle, but can I sit here?"

Inspector Anand looked up. A young plump girl of medium height was standing across from him, one hand already resting on the back of the chair on the other side of the table. She had a beautiful round face, large dark eyes, and black curly hair plaited into one long tail that hung down her back. She was dressed in a pale orange salwar-kameez outfit, and a canvas bag was slung across one shoulder.

"By all means, please do sit down," the Inspector said, gesturing towards the empty chair.

"All the other tables are taken," the girl said, by way of explanation, as she seated herself. She slipped her heavy canvas bag off her shoulder, and laying it on the table, extracted a lunch box from it. The bag appeared to contain textbooks and notebooks.

"You bring lunch from home? Don't you like the food here?" he asked her, smiling, as the girl opened up her lunchbox.

"Oh, the food here is very good," she replied. "But my mother always insists on packing me lunch. She is of the firm belief that all food outside is bad and can do terrible things to one's stomach." She lowered her voice conspiratorially, and eyes twinkling, added: "But once in a while, after eating what my mother has packed for me, I get myself some of the yummy snacks they make here."

"I used to do the same thing when I was in college," Inspector Anand laughed. Then becoming serious, he said: "Please don't think this is an impudent question, but did you feel quite safe in asking to sit with someone who is after all a complete stranger?"

"You looked quite respectable, uncle," the young girl replied, calmly chomping her food. "Besides, look around you — the place is crowded. If you tried to do anything, I would only have to cry for help once, and a dozen or so of the gallant young men around would fall on you and give you a good thrashing."

"That is so true," the Inspector said, laughing again. "To give you further comfort, let me say that you remind me a great deal of my own daughter."

"See — I could tell that you were a respectable family man!" the girl said triumphantly.

Inspector Anand sat sipping his chai, wondering how to bring the subject around to Thakshak, while his young companion continued to eat her lunch. He tried overhear some of the chatter at nearby tables, hoping to hear some mention of that youth, but the conversations appeared to be mostly about various films running in theaters at the present time, upcoming cricket matches, coupled with the usual complaints about most of the professors, and how hard some of the courses were.

A loud uproar at one of the tables at the far end of the room attracted his attention. Thakshak was standing at a table, clapping some of the seated students on the back, and talking and laughing loudly. The Inspector's young companion followed his gaze and a frown came over her face.

"Pay no attention to them, uncle," she said. "That is the rowdy bunch."

"Who is that boy standing there, talking at the top of his voice?" Inspector Anand asked, pretending not to know who it was.

"Oh, that is a boy named Thakshak," she replied. Her frown deepened. "He is the worst of the lot — always up to no good! He drinks and gambles, makes crude remarks to girls, and is a really bad character."

"I see. Why don't the college authorities do anything about him?"

"I heard that his uncle is some big-shot judge," the girl replied. "So naturally the authorities leave him alone."

She finished her lunch, and began gathering up her things. She stood up, and slung the canvas bag over one shoulder, and said, "My next class is due to begin soon, so I have to get back. It was nice talking to you, uncle."

"It was nice talking to you too, my dear," Inspector Anand said, sincerely.

After she left, the Inspector continued to sit at the table, ruminating. He had managed to corroborate what Mrs. Pillai had told him about Thakshak. But while he was, as the evidence indicated, a wild young man, did that mean he would go so far as to murder his own uncle? And what was his motive? His uncle was paying for his college education, such as it was. The young man appeared to be focused only on having a good time. If he killed his uncle, that fun lifestyle would vanish.

Inspector Anand sighed and got to his feet. Better get back to the office. He would send out a couple of constables to investigate if any suspicious looking characters were seen hanging around the judge's residence on the night of the murder. He did not have much hope, but one never knew. With luck, some new evidence might unexpectedly turn up.

As the Inspector made his way to the wide doors that led outside, Thakshak caught sight of him and froze. One of his seated friends asked jovially, "Whatever is the matter, Thakshak? You look like you just saw a ghost!"

*What the hell is the Inspector doing here?* thought Thakshak. With a hasty, mumbled goodbye to his friends, who were left staring at each other in surprise, he dashed after the retreating figure of Inspector Anand, now making his way out through the wide doors of the canteen building.

The Inspector, walking down the gravel path leading from the canteen building towards the lot where his car was parked, heard hurrying footsteps behind him, coming fast. He turned around sharply and came face to face with a breathless Thakshak.

"What are you doing here?" the young man burst out.

Inspector Anand raised a quizzical eyebrow. "Surely I can come to the college campus if I want to, can I not? I did not see any sign that said 'Only students can enter the premises'."

"No, no, of course not," mumbled Thakshak, his eyes darting this way and that. Then he seemed to make up his mind. "But let us not stand and talk here. Why don't we go over there," and he pointed to an unoccupied stone bench under the shade of a large tree, about a foot away from the tall brick wall that formed the outer boundary of the college campus. "I have something to tell you," he said, and hurriedly set off towards the spot. Inspector Anand followed at a more leisurely pace.

When he arrived at the bench, Thakshak was already seated, head bowed, hands clasped together, and staring at the ground beneath his feet. The Inspector seated himself next to the young man and waited.

For a few minutes Thakshak did not say anything. Then, swallowing hard, he said: "I was not being entirely truthful, Inspector, when I told you what happened in my uncle's office room that night, when he was murdered."

Inspector Anand kept his face impassive, and said: "Go on."

"The fact is, I did see someone at the window when the shot was fired."

"I see. Why did you say that you saw no one, when I questioned you that night?"

"It was just a quick glimpse, and I couldn't be sure," Thakshak said. "I had my back to the window when I heard the sound of a shot being fired and my uncle was hit in the chest. I was frozen with shock for a few moments. I swung around, and I think I saw a face quickly pulling back."

"Can you describe this face?" asked the Inspector.

The young man shook his head. "I caught the barest glimpse."

The Inspector waited for a few minutes, but Thakshak did not add anything more, just continued staring at the ground, his hands clasped together. He did not turn his head to meet the Inspector's gaze.

Finally the Inspector rose to his feet and said, "I think you're still not telling me everything. Remember what I said to you that night - withholding evidence from a police officer is against the law, and could get you in serious trouble. So think seriously about that. If you recall anything further, call me at once."

# Chapter 11

Next morning, Inspector Anand had hardly been in his office for an hour, when he received a phone call from a good friend of his, K.S. Rani. Widowed at a young age, she had by the dint of perseverance and hard work, built up a successful jewelry business, aptly named Rani's Jewelers. Her shop wasn't large, but had over the years developed a good reputation as the place one went to for quality diamonds.

"Ashok, I need your help," Rani said. "Can you come over right away?"

"Why, what on earth's the matter?" the Inspector asked. He knew Rani well enough to be aware that she would not sound so worried nor ask for his urgent assistance unless it was something serious.

"A valuable diamond has been stolen," she said, getting right to the point. "But I don't know how. And I have a suspect right here, who needs to be searched."

"That sounds serious. But I would like more detail. Why don't you tell me everything that happened, right from the beginning."

"Yes, sorry, Ashok," Rani said. The Inspector heard her take a deep breath. "When I opened up my shop this morning at 9:30 am, I found a customer already waiting outside. An old gentleman, well dressed, and leaning on a walking cane. He was the only customer waiting. He walked in with difficulty, his right leg seemed quite weak, and he had to use his cane for support. My son Ganesh assisted him to a chair in front of the counter. He said that he wanted to see some unset diamonds, and he would later pick out a ring and have us set it for him. There were some in a display case. He said he found it difficult to lean forward in his chair to see them properly, and since he found it difficult to walk, he asked if we could take out the tray from the display case and bring it over to where he sitting. Ganesh took out the tray and showed it to the customer. He looked over the diamonds we had in that tray, and said he didn't like any of them, and asked if we had anything more valuable. He said that he was wealthy, and prepared to pay a high price. I keep a tray of really valuable diamonds in a large safe in my office in the back of the store. I decided to show him those diamonds."

Rani took another deep breath, and continued: "Ganesh brought out the tray and took it over to where the old man was sitting. The customer leaned forward to inspect the diamonds more closely, and suddenly seemed to lose his balance. He clutched at one of Ganesh's arms for support, causing the tray of valuable diamonds to tilt forward, and many of the diamonds spilled out onto the floor. Poor Ganesh! He was aghast. He dropped to his knees, set the tray on the floor, and started picking up the diamonds, which were scattered all over. I immediately ran to the front doors of the shop and closed and locked them."

"Were there any other customers in the shop at that time?" interrupted Inspector Anand.

"No, no else besides this old man had come in. We usually don't get any customers this early on a weekday. Our business typically picks up only after lunchtime."

"I see. Go on."

Rani continued, "I went to help Ganesh. My daughter in law also came to help. Together, we collected the diamonds and put them back in the tray. At that point, we discovered that one very valuable diamond was missing. So we searched again, every nook and cranny of the store."

"What was the customer doing at that time?" asked the Inspector.

"He was sitting in his chair. He apologized profusely for causing the accident."

"Did you have any other employees in the store?"

"Not at that particular time. I do employ another young man who helps out with customers, but he doesn't come in till the afternoon. I mainly use him in the evenings, because that's when the bulk of our business is transacted."

"So, to be perfectly clear, at the time the diamonds were spilt onto the floor, the only people inside the store were yourself, your son, your daughter in law, and the customer."

"That's correct," Rani said. "Ashok, we have looked everywhere, but we can't find that diamond! I hate to suspect this customer, but who else could have taken it? I trust my son and daughter-in-law totally. I am calling from my office in the back of the store, by the way, so the customer can't hear. Oh, can you come right away?" Rani's voice sounded close to tears.

"Don't mind this question, but do you really think this old man could have somehow taken the diamond?"

"Who else? Besides, he's not that old, probably in his mid sixties, I would say. Perhaps when the tray tilted, one of the diamonds fell into his lap, and he quietly pocketed it without anyone noticing. When the diamonds scattered to the floor, Ganesh immediately dropped to his knees, and I had rushed to the front door to lock it, so the customer could have easily pocketed the diamond that fell into his lap without anyone seeing. Can you come and search him? You know how to do it properly. I'll keep him here, showing him various pieces of jewelry and other diamonds, and prolonging the process, till you arrive."

Inspector Anand thought swiftly. He had sent two constables out this morning to investigate if any suspicious looking characters had been seen hanging around Judge Mohan Pillai's residence on Saturday night around the time of the murder, but the likelihood was that they would not report back with their findings until later in the day. Going over to Rani's Jewelers and searching the suspect would take him away from his office for an hour and a half or two hours at the most. He thought of all the times when Rani had helped his wife and him, and how supportive she had been after his wife had passed away. Yes, he should help her now.

"I'll come over at once," he said.

The police jeep pulled up in front of Rani's Jewelers twenty minutes later. Inspector Anand jumped out and ran up the short flight of steps leading to the large double glass doors of the shop and tapped on the glass.

The Inspector saw Rani getting to her feet and hurrying towards the front doors, which she unlocked to let him in. He saw relief on her face.

The interior, with two ceiling fans whirring quietly overhead, provided a welcome coolness from the outside heat. Inspector Anand focused his attention on the well-dressed man with white hair and luxuriant beard, seated on a chair in front of one the display counters. The fingers of both hands were wrapped around the L-shaped brass handle of a wooden cane, and he was leaning on the cane as he peered at a tray being held by Ganesh. As the uniformed figure of Inspector Anand approached him, the customer raised his head and frowned.

"What is the meaning of this?" he asked Rani, sharply. "Why is a police officer here?"

"You remember when some of the diamonds fell to the floor?" Rani said. "When we finished gathering them all up, we found that there was one valuable one missing."

"What has that to do with me?" demanded the customer, testily. "It could have easily rolled off somewhere." He waved his left hand around the shop.

"We searched very thoroughly," Rani said. "As you can see, the floor is polished tile. It was actually not that hard to locate all the diamonds that had fallen — except one."

Inspector Anand stepped forward. "Your name, sir?" he asked.

"Sivan Makan," said the customer.

"Mr. Makan, I would like to search you."

"This is an outrage!" Sivan Makan said, puffing out his cheeks. "To be treated like a common criminal! Is this how you take care of your customers?" he demanded, turning to Rani.

Rani turned pale, but stood her ground admirably. "Mr. Makan, I am really sorry, but I have no choice."

"Very well! I prefer to leave here without a stain on my character, so Mr. Police Officer, you can search me."

"Why don't you use my office in the back?" suggested Rani. "That way, you can have some privacy."

Mr. Makan struggled to his feet, and using his cane for support, made his way slowly to the back of the store, accompanied by Inspector Anand. The Inspector was now assailed by doubts. If the customer had slipped a diamond into his one of his pockets when no one was looking, would he have consented to a search so readily?

After half an hour, the Inspector had to concede defeat. He had searched Mr. Makan as thoroughly as he could think of. Even his shoes had not been spared. But there was no trace of the missing diamond.

Feeling dejected, he accompanied slow moving Mr. Makan back to the showroom. As they came out of the back office, Rani's pale, strained face looked directly at the Inspector. He shook his head. Poor Rani! This would not be good for business. Mr. Makan would no doubt vindictively spread the story of how he had been detained and searched.

But a nebulous thought was tugging at the back of Inspector Anand's mind, a feeling that he had overlooked something. Oddly enough, his mind kept going back to a Bollywood film he had seen in his younger days, a hugely successful crime thriller that contained a scene which revealed an ingenious hiding place for a cache of stolen diamonds...

That was it! His mind latched on to what he had overlooked when performing his search.

Mr. Sivan Makan was almost at the front glass doors of the shop, and Rani was getting ready to open them to let him out.

"Stop!" yelled Inspector Anand.

Rani stared at him, surprised. Mr. Makan stood stock still, then swung around.

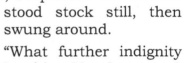

"What further indignity is this, Mr. Inspector? How long am I to be subject to this kind of abuse? I will have you know, I am well connected, and I will most certainly complain to those in charge."

The Inspector said: "Mr. Makan, when performing my search earlier, I overlooked one item."

"One item? What do you mean? What one item?"

"Your cane," said Inspector Anand.

Was it his imagination, or did a flash of fear quickly cross the old man's face?

"My cane?  Really, Inspector, now you are going too far!  I really must protest."

"Nonetheless, I wish to examine it," said Inspector Anand, grimly.  "Ganesh, please escort Mr. Makan to a chair.  Now, sir, your cane, if you please."

The customer opened his mouth as if to protest, then slumped back in his chair and silently handed the cane over.  In appearance it was a thick wooden cane with  a polished brass L-shaped handle on top, slightly curved.  The bottom end of the wooden shaft, where the cane would meet the ground when in use, was covered by a rubber cap.  To all appearances, it was there to protect the end of  the wooden shaft from wear and tear.

The Inspector examined the brass handle carefully.  On the underside of the handle was a tiny button, so small that it could easily be overlooked.  Pointing the cane downwards, he pressed the button, and the rubber cap at the end of the cane swung open.  A glittering diamond fell on to the shiny polished tile floor with a clatter.

A collective gasp went up from Rani, Ganesh and his wife.  Ganesh bent down and picked up the diamond reverently.

After handcuffing and marching the unfortunate Sivan Makan to the police jeep and placing him in the back seat in custody of the driver, Inspector Anand went back inside Rani's Jewelers.  Rani was tearful in her thanks.

"A very ingenious scheme," said the Inspector.  "I strongly suspect that he has done this sort of thing before. Overbalancing and clutching Ganesh's arm, causing the diamonds to spill onto the floor, no doubt was done on purpose. Then, while all of you were distracted and scrambling about, he used that little button in the handle to neatly scoop up one of the diamonds with the rubber cap into a small hollow at the bottom of the cane shaft. His cane must have been specially designed for that purpose. It would have been done so quickly and quietly that none of you would have noticed. He would have been careful to choose a moment when all of you had your backs to him. You would not have been watching him, because at that point, you had all thought that it was just an accident, and you had no reason to suspect him."

# Chapter 12

After seeing Mr. Makan safely locked up in one of the cells at headquarters, Inspector Anand filled out the FIR, charge sheet, and other paperwork for what he had mentally started referring to as The Missing Diamond Case. He reflected ironically that the episode might have even elicited a rare congratulatory remark from Sherlock Holmes himself ("Well done, Inspector! I am beginning to entertain some hopes, however feeble, for the abilities of the police force.")

Then his mind went back to the big case he was handling, the murder of Judge Mohan Pillai, and his exultant thoughts collapsed in an instant. He was making so little progress! True, he had not been idle, he had questioned those involved thoroughly, gathered a good deal of information, and eliminated a key suspect — Rajakkan — but in terms of identifying a murderer, he was no closer than he had been on Saturday night.

Come to think of it, where were the two constables he had sent out this morning to gather information? But a quick glance at his wristwatch told him that it was only 1:00 pm. In all likelihood they wouldn't return and make their report until the evening.

He realized at that point that he was very hungry. Perhaps he should go and eat lunch. The easiest place to go to was the headquarters canteen. The food there wasn't bad.

It being lunchtime, the canteen was crowded. After collecting his order, the Inspector stood with his tray of food, scanning the room for an empty seat. Then he spotted Inspector Bhasakran sitting by himself at a small table in one corner. He made his way there.

"Ashok!" Bhaskaran said, with evident pleasure, and then immediately asked: "Were you able to locate Rajakkan and talk to him? I hope you have your case solved already, and Rajakkan is locked up in one of our cells."

Inspector Anand shook his head ruefully, and brought Bhaskaran up to date with the events that had transpired with Rajakkan.

"That's too bad," Bhaskaran said. "Now it looks like you will have to start searching for a suspect all over again. Maybe someone who saw the whole thing will turn up."

Inspector Anand hesitated, then said: "Actually, I do have one key witness," and he told him all about Thakshak.

"Why didn't you tell me this before?" demanded Bhaskaran. "Why, if you feel like he's keeping something from you, the solution is simple. Bring him in here and we'll get the truth out of him. You know we have ways of making a suspect talk."

Inspector Anand said, quietly, "You know that I don't subscribe to those methods."

Bhaskaran shook his head sadly. "That's the problem with you, Ashok. You're too much of a goody two-shoes. Well, it's your case. I wish you luck. I'll keep my eyes and ears open, will let you know if I hear anything."

They made their way out of the canteen and parted ways. As he walked back to his office, Inspector Anand thought about what Bhaskaran had said. Was he being too principled? He had suspected from the beginning that Thakshak was not being entirely truthful, that he was hiding something. Should he do what Bahaskar had suggested, bring the youth in and extract the truth by any means, foul or fair? He was well aware that brutal methods were often employed to extract information from a suspect, although officially they were not supposed to. Unfortunately, many police officers believed that unlawful methods like beatings and even torture were necessary tactics of crime investigation and law enforcement.

He had no sooner than seated himself at his desk when his phone rang.

"Inspector Anand speaking," he said into the receiver.

"Ah! The famous Inspector Ashok Anand, one of the few honest and decent officers in the Trivandrum police force," said an unknown voice, jovially.

The Inspector, still smarting from his colleague's description of him as a 'goody two-shoes', felt himself flush with anger. "Who is this?" he demanded.

"Who I am is not important," replied the unknown caller. "I heard that you are working on the Judge Pillai murder case."

"How do you know this?"

"Oh, Inspector, it is my business to know such things," said the unseen voice, chuckling. "But anyway, I might be able to help you."

Inspector Anand's pulse quickened. Perhaps this would turn out to be the break he had been hoping for. "Go on," he said.

"I can tell you this much," went on the caller. "None of the gang leaders in Trivandrum were involved in this murder."

The Inspector's heart sank. If this was true, it made his task much more difficult. "Are you sure?" he asked.

"Who can be sure of anything in this life?" asked the voice, enigmatically. "But yes, I am reasonably sure."

"Could it be someone else, acting independently, and who had a grudge against the judge?"

"You mean like Rajakkan?" asked the unseen caller. "But no, Rajakkan did not commit this crime. I heard what you did to help him, by the way."

"You appear to be singularly well informed," said the Inspector, sardonically.

"I have to be, Inspector. It is the best way to survive."

"If you are so well informed, perhaps you can tell me who committed this murder?"

"Sorry, Inspector, I cannot do all your work for you. I can only tell you what I have heard. I hope I have eliminated some possibilities. The rest is up to you."

And Inspector Anand heard the click of a telephone receiver being replaced back on its cradle.

He put down the receiver at his end, leaned back in his chair, and stared thoughtfully into space. Who could this caller be? Based on the things he had said, he was either a gang leader, or someone well connected with the gangs in the city.

Trivandrum was on the whole a peaceful town, but the Inspector was well aware that it had its share of organized crime engaged in an assorted variety of illegal activities: bootlegging, smuggling, prostitution, and the like.

If the caller was correct, then none of the gangs had been involved in the murder of Judge Mohan Pillai. But it still left open the possibility that it could have been carried out by some felon acting on his own, someone who had run afoul of the judge.

He heard the sound of heavy boots thumping on the concrete floor just outside his office, and the two constables he had sent out that morning to investigate if any suspicious looking characters had been seen hanging around the judge's residence on the night of the murder, entered. They had a firm grip on the arms of a thin boy with a grimy face and large round eyes, dressed in a dirty short sleeve shirt and short trousers. He could not have been more than eight to ten years old, and he looked terrified.

"Who is this?" asked Inspector Anand, as the two constables brought the boy to a standstill in front of his desk.

The more senior of the two, old, large Constable Chacko, looked excited. "An eyewitness, sir! He saw something suspicious around Judge Pillai's residence on Saturday night." He gave the boy a little push, and growled at him: "Tell Mr. Inspector what you saw."

The boy hung his head and looked at floor in silence.

"Speak!" barked Chacko, raising one of his massive arms threateningly. "Tell the Inspector what you told us, or I will give you a thrashing!"

The boy burst into tears.

The big constable raised his hand, but before it could descend on the boy, Inspector Anand intervened. "Chacko!" he said, sharply. "Why don't you and Constable Ketu wait outside while I question the young fellow."

"Yes, Inspector," Chacko gave the lad a look of disgust and clumped out in his heavy boots, followed by Ketu.

Inspector Anand rummaged in the right-hand drawer of his desk and brought out a handful of toffees in their shiny twisted wrappers, and laid them on the desk in front of his young visitor. "Take as many as you want," he said, gently.

The boy peered suspiciously at the Inspector, and saw that he was smiling and nodding. He grabbed a handful of the sweets and stuffed them into his trouser pocket.

"What is your name?" asked Inspector Anand.

"Manu, sir," said the boy.

"Now, Manu, you needn't be afraid," said the Inspector. "Tell me what you told the two constables."

"I won't get into trouble if I tell?" asked Manu.

"No, you will not get

into trouble. You will actually be helping me if you can provide any information."

Thus reassured, Manu said: "I was walking along the street where Judge Pillai lives, on Saturday night, after delivering an order of chai to one of the houses. I saw a man trying to climb over the wall of the Judge's house."

"Can you describe him?" asked Inspector Anand.

"It was dark, and I did not get a good look," said the boy. "But I could tell that he was a large man."

"Did you see his face?"

Manu shook his head. "Not clearly."

"Did he get over the wall?" asked the Inspector.

"No. When he spotted me, he jumped down and started coming towards me. So I took to my heels and ran off as fast as I could. I am a fast runner," Manu added proudly.

"When he turned and started coming towards you, you must have seen his face."

"All I saw was that he had a big beard and curly hair."

"Anything else? What kind of face was it? Round? Thin? Long?"

Manu pondered for a few minutes, gazing into the distance in an effort at recall. Inspector Anand knew that it was not easy for a youngster like him to describe a person's face; his experience had shown that even adults had a surprising amount of difficulty with accurate descriptions.

"He had a large face," Manu said finally. The Inspector waited for a few minutes, but Manu did not add anything.

Inspector Anand said kindly: "Thank you, Manu. What you have told me might help us catch a bad man."

The boy flushed with pride. To be thanked by no less a great person than a police inspector! He instantly revised his prior long-held belief that all policemen were bad and corrupt. Of course, that large Constable Chacko had been rough with him, but this nice police inspector had made up for that. He felt the toffees in his pants pocket and sighed with contentment.

"I can have one of the constables take you home," the Inspector said. "Where do you live?"

"Actually, I have to return to work in my father's chai shop," Manu said. "That is where the constables picked me up. They stopped in to have some chai and I overheard them talking about Judge Pillai's murder, so I told them what I had seen."

On an impulse, Inspector Anand said: "I will take you there myself."

As they made their way towards the Inspector's car, Manu's eyes grew round. "That is an old German car!" he blurted out. "Very rare."

Inspector Anand glanced at him quizzically. "You seem to know quite a lot about cars."

"I can identify every make and model on the streets," said Manu proudly.

The Inspector seated Manu in the front passenger seat and had him provide the directions to his father's tea shop. It turned out to be located at the end of the street where Judge Pillai had his residence, where the quiet residential street intersected with the busy main road.

There was no parking space to be had in the immediate vicinity of the tea stall, and the Inspector had to park his car around the corner. He got out and followed Manu, who was dashing excitedly ahead. Typical of the majority of such tea stalls, it was small, with only one rough wooden table with two benches on either side, which at the time was fully occupied. Most of the customers were standing on the pavement, drinking their steaming hot glasses of chai, and chatting with each other. Inspector Anand noted that, despite its small size, the tea shop appeared to be doing a thriving business. Behind the counter a lean middle aged man with a bushy mustache was ladling out glasses of milky sweet-spicy chai from a huge tureen. An aromatic smell of brewing tea mixed with cardamom, ginger, cinnamon, and other spices filled the air.

"My father makes the best chai around here," said Manu, proudly. "Please have a glassful." He ran forward, calling out loudly: "Achan! A glass of chai for the Inspector!"

The customers gathered around the front of the tea stall parted to let them through. Some of them stared curiously at the tall figure of the Inspector. Others teasingly said: "So, Manu, you have made friends with the police, have you? You think that will help when you get in trouble?" There was general laughter all around.

The man behind the counter filled a tall glass with chai, handed it to the Inspector, and then said dourly to Manu: "So you have finally come back? Going off with those two constables like that, and leaving me to deal with all these customers by myself."

"But, father, I had to give evidence," said Manu, puffing out his chest importantly.

"I am sure the police can manage without your help," said his father.

"Actually, Manu was most helpful," said Inspector Anand. "You have raised a good boy."

Manu's father looked pleased. "I am glad the boy was able to help. I have taught him to always tell the truth."

"That is very important. By the way, this chai is excellent."

"I use the best ingredients only," Manu's father said proudly.

"Manu seems very interested in cars," mentioned the Inspector. "When he grows up, perhaps you can send him for training to be a mechanic?"

"But then who will take care of my tea stall?" demanded the father. "When I get too old, Manu will have to take over. It is a good business."

Inspector Anand was about to say that the boy should be allowed to follow his own interests, then thought better of it, and remained silent. Who was he to tell these people how they should run their life? He reflected that the father was merely expressing the desire of small (and large) business owners all over India, that their sons take over the business when they got too old. Better to let Manu tell his father himself, when the time came; that is, if he wanted to. Who knew, an older Manu might feel that the tea stall was a very good enterprise and be happy running it. The Inspector had read somewhere that a busy tea stall like this one could provide the owner with much more in net profit per month than the salary paid at many entry level jobs.

He finished his chai and paid for it, over the protests of Manu's father. He decided that since he was so close to Judge Pillai's residence, he would go over there and give Mrs. Pillai a quick update on the progress of the case thus far. But as drove up to the house, he saw a number of cars parked in front. Evidently, friends, neighbors, and in all likelihood, relatives had come to express their condolences and provide whatever comfort and help they could to the widow. He decided that he would not intrude at this time; he had made little concrete progress on the case, anyway, and an update could be postponed until he had something more hopeful to tell her.

It was getting to be late evening, with shadows lengthening across the streets now crowded with vehicles and people returning home from work. Inspector Anand decided, like them, to go home; he could begin his search for the bearded large man with curly hair the next day. He reflected that there must be hundreds, perhaps thousands of men in Trivandrum answering to that description.

He eventually made it back home, and let himself into his dark, empty house. He felt tired and despondent.

# Chapter 13

Inspector Anand was fond of reading. He liked nothing better than to sit in his favorite armchair after dinner, pick up a good novel or some magazine, and read until bedtime. He found it to be a very effective way of reducing the stress that was unavoidable in his job. He was currently reading "The Godfather", a thrilling, well written book about a mafia family based in New York. An hour of reading brought him to a passage in the book that made him sit up straight, eyes gleaming. The section he had just read had given him an idea pertaining to the murder of Judge Mohan Pillai. Would this provide the solution to his very difficult case? There was only one way to find out, and that was to proceed to the Pillai residence and investigate. Should he go there right away? No, it was getting on for ten o'clock at night, and there was no harm in waiting till tomorrow morning, since the judge's office room was locked, and he possessed the only key, so no one else could go in and remove the evidence that he now thought he would find. No point in disturbing the household at this late hour.

Inspector Anand slept badly that night. His mind refused to be still, repeatedly going over and over his hypothesis, which if proven correct, could solve the case. He finally fell into a troubled sleep close to dawn, and when he woke up, it was much later than he wished. He hurriedly took a shower, got dressed in his uniform and drove to headquarters, to commandeer a police jeep and driver. If his theory was correct, he would need the vehicle to make an arrest soon after searching the office room of the Pillai residence.

Arriving there, and after being admitted by the old watchman, Inspector Anand hurried up the gravel driveway. The judge's Ambassador car was parked in its usual spot, but there was no sign of Balram. Perhaps he was in the kitchen, eating his breakfast, or doing some work in the rear garden. The front door of the house was closed, but he could hear voices within, both male and female. Some relatives or friends must have arrived early or stayed overnight, which would not be surprising. He crossed the veranda and knocked on the front door.

Instantly he could hear the conversation inside cease. After a few moments, the door was opened by a short, plump, pompous looking man, whose facial features resembled Mrs. Pillai's a great deal. Seeing the Inspector in his uniform, he called over his shoulder, "The police are here," and stepped aside to let him enter.

The Inspector noted that in addition to Mrs. Pillai, who was seated on the sofa, and the short plump man who had opened the door, there was a thin middle aged lady with a lively intelligent face seated in one of the armchairs.

Mrs. Pillai said eagerly: "Ah! Inspector Anand! Any progress?"

"Actually, madam, I've come to search the office room again," the Inspector said. "I have a hunch that I'll find a piece of evidence there that will solve the case." I hope I'm right, he silently prayed.

Mrs. Pillai looked skeptical. "If you could not find anything in your earlier searches, why do you think you'll find something now? But by all means, please go ahead and conduct another search. By the way, this is my brother Balu and his wife Ganga."

"Pleased to meet you, Inspector," Balu said, coming forward and shaking hands. "Please go ahead and do whatever you need to get to the bottom of this terrible business. What is Trivandrum coming to, when a notable judge can be murdered like this, in cold blood? The killer must be caught, Inspector, and made an example of!" He lifted his round little chin defiantly.

"Oh, stop your over-acting, Balu," his wife Ganga said unexpectedly, in an amused tone. "I am sure the police are aware of the importance of solving this crime. Please ignore him, Inspector. Balu tends to get carried away."

Balu opened his mouth to protest, but Inspector Anand hastily cut in. "Actually, Mrs. Pillai, I was wondering if I could make use of Balram for a few minutes? I want him to act as a witness when I conduct my search, so that I don't get accused by some clever defence lawyer later, of planting evidence."

"Very wise of you, Inspector!" cried Balu. "But there is no need to trouble Balram! I can act as your witness."

"Very well, sir," the Inspector said. "If you don't mind, I'd like to begin at once."

Inspector Anand made his way along the veranda to the office room, unlocked the door and entered, followed by Balu, who could barely disguise his air of self-importance. "Please come with me, sir," the Inspector said, crossing the office room and stepping into the small adjoining bathroom. He turned on the electric light, took a pair of plastic gloves from his trousers pocket and pulled them on over his hands. He walked over to the toilet tank, took off its porcelain lid, and peered inside, with Balu watching in pop-eyed amazement from the doorway.

Inside the toilet tank, lying at the bottom of the water, was a gun.

The Inspector, who had been holding his breath, let it out with huge sigh of relief. His hunch had paid off. He reached in with his right hand, covered with the plastic glove, and lifted out the gun, dripping with water.

Balu's eyes grew big and round. "Inspector!" he squealed. "That is a gun! But - but, how did it get there? What does this mean?"

"It was hidden there by the murderer," said Inspector Anand, grimly. He pulled out a clear plastic bag from his pocket, dropped the gun in it, and sealed the bag. "Excuse me sir, but I have have to go and make an arrest, right away."

"Yes-yes, of course," stammered Balu, backing out of the bathroom hurriedly.

Just then, Balram entered the office room, saying, "Madam said you needed me, Inspector sahib." He stopped when he caught sight of the Inspector emerging from the little bathroom, holding the plastic bag with the gun in it. For a moment, Balram's usual calmness deserted him, and his eyes opened a little wide at the sight, but he quickly regained control of himself. He asked, quietly, "Is that the murder weapon?"

"I am pretty sure it is," said Inspector Anand. "I'll have it tested, of course, to make sure that the bullet that killed Judge Pillai matches this gun. I rather think it will."

"Where did you find it?" asked Balram.

"It was hidden in the toilet tank."

Balram's eyes filled with an infinite sadness. "Thakshak put it there?"

"I don't see who else could have," the Inspector replied. "He must have got the idea of hiding the gun there when he went into the bathroom to fetch the towel. That explains his delay in opening the door of the office room."

Balram shook his turbaned head sorrowfully. "I was hoping that it would not be the boy, that it would be someone who had fired a shot through the window. Poor Mrs. Pillai is going be very upset."

"I was hoping it would be someone else, too," said the Inspector. "But now, Balram, you know that I have to do my duty and arrest him."

"I understand, Inspector sahib."

Inspector Anand strode out of the office room, and at that precise moment, Thakshak came climbing up the steps to the veranda. His Vespa scooter was, as usual, parked on the driveway just inside the front gates.

He took one look at the Inspector carrying the plastic bag with the gun in it clearly visible, wheeled around, and took to his heels.

"Stop!" yelled Inspector Anand. "Stop him!" he shouted to the old watchman, who was seated on his little stool just inside the big iron gates.

But by the time the old fellow had stopped gaping and struggled to his feet from his stool, Thakshak had mounted his Vespa scooter, kick-started it into sputtering life, and sped through the front gates to the street beyond. He made a sharp left turn onto the street, and accelerated his scooter towards the main road some two hundred yards away.

Inspector Anand sprinted through the gates to the police jeep parked outside on the street. The driver, Constable Kurian, who had been enjoying a quiet smoke under the shade of a tree, had heard the commotion inside the compound but had not been sure who the Inspector was trying to stop when the Vespa scooter had raced past him on to the street. But he when he saw the Inspector came running out of the front gates, he had enough presence of mind to spring into the jeep and start up the engine.

Inspector Anand clambered on to the passenger seat. Balram came running up and said, "Please let me come with you, Inspector. Perhaps I can help."

Inspector Anand hesitated. Strictly speaking, he should not admit a civilian into a police vehicle that was about to give chase to a suspect. On the other hand, Balram was a former military man and a trained bodyguard, and knowing Thakshak well, he might be able to provide insight as to where that young man might be headed. He had to make up his mind quickly, every precious second meant that Thakshak would be getting further away.

He said to Balram: "Get in the back seat."

The police jeep set off in hot pursuit. The orange colored Vespa, with Thakshak astride, was already some hundred yards down the street. They saw him arrive at the intersection with the main road, and then turn left into the hooting, honking mass of auto rickshaws, cars, big lumbering buses, and bicycles. Arriving at the intersection a few minutes later, Constable Kurian expertly swung the police jeep into the seething mass of traffic, and honked furiously at vehicles, bicycles, and pedestrians to get out of the way.

Where was Thakshak headed for? The Inspector took a deep breath and forced himself to think calmly and logically. Thakshak would know that he was a wanted man, so that ruled out the possibility of him heading back to his hostel to pack up what he could into a suitcase. He would in all probability try to head out of town as quickly as possible, and make for one of the other big cities in the state, like Ernakulam or Cochin. It was unlikely that he would head to a small town, where he could be more easily traced. He might even try to leave the state entirely, and head for a big city in a neighboring state, like Bangalore or Chennai, and try to get lost among their teeming millions. But would he try to head out of town on his scooter right away? No, Thakshak would be aware that the top speed of his Vespa scooter was far below that of the police jeep, and once they left the center of the city, and were on an open road

110

with little traffic, the police jeep would easily catch up.

Would he head for the airport? No, too risky: who knew when the next flight out of town would be? Moreover, buying an airline ticket at the last minute would not be easy; what if all the flights were fully booked up?

Would Thakshak head to the main train station? But no, again there might be too long of a wait for the next train out of town.

The central bus terminus? Yes! There were express buses constantly leaving the terminus, headed out of the city to neighbouring towns and even to places as far away as Bangalore and Chennai. And purchasing a bus ticket was easy; no identification was asked for at the counter, one simply handed over the price of the ticket.

Inspector Anand quickly explained his rationale to Balram, who concurred. "Yes, Inspector sahib, you're right, I think that is where he would be headed."

Inspector Anand barked at Kurian: "Head towards the central bus terminus."

He anxiously scanned the mass of vehicles ahead. Then Balram leaned forward and pointed: "Look, there he is!". And sure enough, there was Thakshak, some sixty yards down the road, weaving his orange Vespa scooter through the traffic, zipping in between vehicles, and making far more headway than the police jeep.

In response to Kurian's furious honking and yelling, the traffic in front of the police jeep was reluctantly moving aside to let them through. Then suddenly a big municipal bus, belching black noxious smoke from its tailpipe, cut right in front of them, completely blocking off their view of their quarry. Kurian jammed on his brakes and let loose a stream of choice expletives directed at the unseen bus driver. He redoubled his efforts on the police jeep's horn and swerved the jeep dangerously as tried to get around the big lumbering vehicle in front. He eventually managed to, but after he overtook the bus, yelling at the bus driver as he accelerated by, the orange Vespa scooter, with Thakshak astride, was nowhere to be seen.

Had he turned off into one of the numerous side streets? agonized the Inspector. Perhaps even now Thakshak was retracing his tracks and heading back to his hostel? But no, the youth would surely consider that to be too risky. Let me just stick to my original hunch, that he would head to the bus terminus to grab the first bus out of town. He would know that it would be almost impossible for the Inspector to immediately alert sufficient police stations to stop and search every bus leaving town. He would calculate that it was a risk worth taking.

Due in large part to Kurian's expert and aggressive driving, they arrived at the main bus terminus some ten minutes later.

Inspector Anand sprang out of the police jeep and ran towards the departure bay, accompanied by Balram. Buses were lined up in their slots, most of them with engines already running, ready to take off to their destinations. Lines of passengers were boarding many of the big vehicles, while others were queuing up, waiting to board their particular bus.

I must catch Thakshak, thought the Inspector grimly, as he and Balram ran from one bus to the next, anxiously scanning the lines of passengers. I cannot let him get away! What would the DSP think? It would be a really black mark on my career. He sent up a silent prayer to his late wife.

As if by a miracle, his prayer was answered. He suddenly glimpsed his quarry, climbing aboard a bus just ahead. Thakshak was the last passenger to get on board, and already the bus driver, anxious to be on his way, had put the bus in gear and was slowly backing his large vehicle out of the bay.

The Inspector redoubled his speed. He felt like his lungs would burst from the effort, and the oppressive heat and noxious odor of diesel fumes in the bus terminal were overpowering. With every last ounce of strength that he could summon, he waved his arms frantically and yelled: "Stop! Police!"

For a minute or two it appeared that the bus driver, looking at his side-view mirror and concentrating on backing his big behemoth out of the bay, had not seen him. But then some of the passengers inside spotted the uniformed figure of the police inspector, accompanied by the tall turbaned Sikh, running towards the bus, waving their arms, and yelled at the driver to stop.

The bus driver slammed on the brakes. Thakshak, sitting at the rear of the vehicle, jumped to his feet, and ran towards the front, where the only exit was located. But before he could get off, the panting figure of Inspector Anand arrived at the bus door. The Inspector, with every last ounce of strength he could summon, gripped the young man's arm and held on.

Thakshak frantically tried to shake himself free. But big Balram, who had run up along with the Inspector, stepped behind the youth, wrapped his powerful arms around him, and held him tight.

Gasping, his heart thudding in his chest, Inspector Anand said: "Thakshak Pillai, I hereby arrest you under Section 300 of the Indian Penal Code for the murder of Judge Mohan Pillai..."

With Balram holding him powerless, the Inspector handcuffed the youth and together, they marched him back to the police jeep, pushing through the curious crowd of onlookers who had already gathered around the scene. Thakshak, head hanging, offered no further resistance. They put him on the back seat, with Balram seating himself next to the boy.

"Back to headquarters, Inspector?" asked Kurian.

"Yes."

While Kurian navigated his way through traffic, Inspector Anand turned around in his seat to look at Thakshak. The boy was weeping silently, his head on Balram's broad shoulder. The Sikh had his arms around the youth, and was murmuring, "It's all right, *beta*. It will be all right. I will take care of you."

The Inspector felt a sudden spasm of pity for the boy. He was after all an orphan, and now he was going to prison. He had basically thrown his life away.

"Why did you do it?" Inspector Anand asked him, gently.

Thakshak raised his tear-stained face. "My uncle was cursing me out and calling me all sorts of names, Inspector. He had a terrible temper.

114

When he was calling me names, I could take it, but when he started cursing my father as well, and saying nasty things about him, my anger got out of control. I loved my father. So I started yelling back, and moved around the desk towards my uncle. That frightened him. He pulled open his desk drawer, took out a gun, pointed it at me, and said that he would shoot me if I came any further."

"Did you know that your uncle kept a gun in his desk?" interrupted the Inspector.

"No, I had no idea."

"So, at that point, what did you do?"

"I yelled at him to put the gun down. But he wouldn't! He kept pointing it at me, and his hand was shaking. I was afraid, really afraid, that he would accidentally squeeze the trigger and shoot me. Then I did a very foolish thing." Thakshak paused and gulped. He was staring, unseeingly, into the distance, his eyes full of fear and anguish as he relived the experience. "I leaned forward and grabbed his hand to push the gun away. We struggled, and the gun went off. My uncle reeled back and fell into his armchair. He started bleeding from a wound in his chest. I was stunned and initially, I didn't know what to do. Then I ran to the bathroom, got the towel that was hanging there, and tried to stem the flow of blood.  But it was too late."

He started sobbing again.

Inspector Anand waited for a few minutes, then said, "When you went to the bathroom to get the towel,  was it then that you got the idea of hiding the gun in the toilet tank?"

"Yes, Inspector."

The Inspector took a deep breath, then said, his voice now sharp rather than sombre: "Thakshak, answer me truthfully — did you ever intend to kill your uncle?"

"No, never! Never!  It was an accident, I swear!"

Inspector Anand shook his head sadly. "Don't you realize it would have been far better for you tell me the truth at the very beginning? With it being an accidental shooting, you might have been able to get a verdict of accidental death."

"I was very scared.  I thought no one would believe me and I would be sent to prison."

With his reputation as a wild young man, the Inspector could see why Thakshak would think that the worst would happen to him.  He said, "Look, I'll see what I can do to help you. Under the circumstances, based on what you have told me, I will try to  convince my superiors that this is a case that can be classified under Sec. 80, 'Accidental Death'. However, there remains the fact that you did try to cover up what had happened, and ended up wasting a great deal of police time.  So the Commissioner may decide to have you appear in front of a magistrate or judge. If your case comes up before a fair-minded judge, you might not even get a jail term.  But, because of your initial cover-up, it's also possible that you may be put on probation."

Thakshak raised his tear-stained face. Hope was dawning in his eyes.

"But you need to promise me something," went on the Inspector. "You have to promise me that you will completely reform, that you will pay attention to your studies, and earn your degree. No more gambling and drinking and wild behaviour. Will you promise me that? If not for me, at least do it for your father's sake."

"I promise, Inspector," whispered Thakshak. "I have learnt my lesson."

Inspector Anand turned back around, leaned back in his seat, and closed his eyes. He felt drained, both physically and emotionally. The case was over, and he was glad that it had been an accidental death, and the young man had not carried out a premeditated murder. But it was still a sad business. Perhaps if Judge Mohan Pillai had not had a bad temper, but he had instead counseled the boy, gently but firmly, none of this would have happened. He recalled a quote from *Julius Caesar*: "The fault, dear Brutus, is not in our stars, but in ourselves."

# Epilogue

Inspector Anand sat on his front veranda after dinner that evening, staring into his dark garden. An important case successfully concluded. The DSP had been pleased. But where was the satisfaction he used to feel? Hardly anything seemed to give him joy anymore. After his beloved wife's death, he had been unable to celebrate any of his successes. Perhaps that was not surprising; she had always been willing to listen to him talk about his work, had always supported him through his frustrations and anxieties, and had always cheered his achievements.

His mind went back, as it often did, to the day when he had first seen the girl who would later become his wife. It had been in his sister's house. He had walked into her sitting room through the front door, and there, standing in a corner, was one of the prettiest girls he had ever seen. Subsequent meetings had revealed her to be sweet and intelligent. Their love for each other had grown with each passing year of their wedded life. He had looked forward to spending a great deal of more time with her after he retired, travelling and reveling in the joy of discovering new places together. It did not seem fair that she had been snatched away from him so prematurely.

In the immediate aftermath of his wife's demise, he had plumbed the depths of despair and thought about killing himself. Why should he live when such a beautiful, loving person was no more?

But then he had thought about his two children. They had already lost one parent, and to lose the remaining one soon afterwards would be cruel. He had also thought of his old mother, who had already suffered so much in life. His mother had lost her husband — his father — at a young age, and had to bring up two children on her own, under very difficult conditions. She had carried on. He must do so, too.

Time would gradually ease the pain. He would never ever forget his dear beloved wife, but as the months and years went by, he hoped that he would be able to think about her without feeling the heartache he felt now.

# *Author's Note*

On May 29, 2017 my life as I knew it changed forever. That was the day my dear beloved wife Vidya passed away after a courageous two-year battle with ALS. She was an incredibly pretty, sweet, kind, and caring person. We had been happily married for 38 years. Words are insufficient to describe how much I miss her. Vidya was, and continues to be, the love of my life and my shining star. Her passing away has left a huge void in my life. The sorrow that I feel is more deep than any I have ever felt before.

Ever since I was young, I have been interested in writing fiction. So, about six months after Vidya's passing, I decided to start writing in earnest. Writing has helped me to keep my mind off my grief to some extent. My first book, a collection of short stories set in India, was well received. In this, my second book, I have written a murder mystery because I am a huge fan of the genre. Within the context of a mystery, I have attempted to provide the reader with an insight into the colourful sights, sounds, and characters of southern India. I have also drawn upon my own emotions in describing the grief that the main character, police inspector Ashok Anand, grapples with as he goes about his duties.

My novel is set in 1980, before the advent of mobile phones (aka cell phones in the United States). The primary mode of telephonic communication in those days was via what is now termed 'land lines'. Police officers had to communicate to headquarters via two-way radio in their vehicles.

I hope you enjoy reading my debut mystery novel. If you did enjoy it, please spread the word: let your friends, relatives, co-workers and acquaintances know. Such word of mouth publicity really helps fledgling authors like myself. Also, please be so kind as to post a review on Amazon; that will also help tremendously.

Gopal Ramanan
June, 2019

## Acknowledgments

I would like to thank Gomathy Naranan, who provided invaluable help by catching the typos in the first printing of my book. Typos are the bane of an author's existence; no matter how careful one is while proofreading, some of them manage to slip in under the radar.